POOL OF HORROR

She had barely squatted beside the water when something—a long, scaly, foul-smelling something—emerged from the pool and wrapped itself firmly around her waist. Shadow had just enough time to reflexively reach for her dagger and gulp a last breath before a tremendous jerk toppled her into the stinking muck.

Shadow cut desperately at the tentacle around her waist, horrified to feel others loop around her legs. Her sharp knife barely penetrated the scaled surface, and she felt herself being pulled deeper. She cut through the tentacle at last, only to feel another wrap firmly around her straining chest.

Ace Books by Anne Logston

SHADOW HUNT

Anne Logston

ACE BOOKS, NEW YORK

This book is an Ace original edition,
and has never been previously published.

SHADOW HUNT

An Ace Book / published by arrangement with
the author

PRINTING HISTORY
Ace edition / May 1992

ISBN: 0-441-76007-4

Ace Books are published by The Berkley Publishing Group,
200 Madison Avenue, New York, New York 10016.
The name ''ACE'' and the ''A'' logo
are trademarks belonging to Charter Communications, Inc.

PRINTED IN THE UNITED STATES OF AMERICA

10 9 8 7 6 5 4 3 2 1

For Mom and Dad
Always

SHADOW HUNT

PROLOGUE ═══

The room was dim, lit by scented lamps. The air was redolent with smells: aged wood, expensive oils and incense, fear. Most of the smells emanated from the fat merchant who cowered upon the cushions.

"How—how did you pass my guards?" he whispered, his heavily jeweled hands twisting together.

She shrugged slightly.

"As I passed Rivero's guards. So many guards, Merchant Tomor. So many more than when we spoke last. If I were the suspicious sort, I would imagine you wished to keep me out. And that would be most ungrateful of you, would it not? Most ungrateful." Her slender, black-gloved hands rested, poised, on her thighs as she crouched just inside the doorway.

Tomor's curiosity overcame, for a moment, his nervousness.

"It's done, then?"

The jet eyes never wavered.

"You doubted? It is done, as you wished. Your competitor is dead. It will not be linked to you. He did not deserve what I did to him."

Despite his nervousness, Tomor barked with harsh laughter.

"That troubles you, a paid killer?"

Chin-length, straight black hair shook slightly with her head.

"It does not trouble me. Do you bait me, Merchant Tomor? It would be unwise of you to do that."

She was all in black leather from chin to toe, and lamplight was swallowed, unreflected, in the darkness of her eyes.

"No. No," Tumor said hurriedly. Then he paused. "Did you torture him?"

The barest hint of a smile touched her pale lips.

"No. It was quick, at least." Her eyes were cold. "You stall, Merchant Tomor. I have come for my payment."

Tomor shivered, his hand clenching around the small, black mark in his palm.

"I've paid your hellish price already."

Her head tilted slightly.

"Need I remind you of the rest of our bargain, Merchant Tomor? I was promised ten thousand Suns in gems when the task was completed."

"You've already been paid more than enough for such a task," Tomor shuddered.

Amusement tinged her voice.

"How typical of you, Merchant Tomor, that you would not balk at giving a part of your life, but a part of your purse is held so dear."

Tomor visibly mustered his courage.

"You have no proof of our agreement, no contract."

"What use is a contract to me?" Her voice was still smooth, but a hint of steel had entered into it. "I am no paid knife of the Aconite Circle. Contracts are for those bargains to be enforced by others, not for bargains whispered in dark rooms. Those bargains I must enforce myself, as I have done, as I will do. Will you pay? Take care, Merchant Tomor. You are less safe than you think. Will you pay?"

Tomor's eyes narrowed.

"You dare threaten me in my own house?" he sneered. "You can't touch me. One word and my guards will be upon you. Eyes watch us even now. You can't threaten me out of my money—"

Even before the last word left his lips, she was at his side, knife at his throat. He trembled. He had not seen her move.

Her voice was cold, caressing.

"No, Merchant Tomor, nor will you threaten me out of mine. There *were* eyes upon you, and guards at your door, but now they sleep past all waking." She briefly glanced at the steel blade of the knife at his throat.

"No. This time, by my own choice."

The knife poised, her eyes never leaving Tomor's, her left hand went to the sheath at her hip. It drew a dagger blacker than night, shining darkly in the lamplight. Its tip replaced the other at Tomor's throat, just under his chin.

Tomor was shaking violently, perspiration dripping from his forehead to the cushions.

"No. I'll pay. I'll pay."

She smiled.

"Yes, Merchant Tomor. You will pay."

Tomor had no time to scream as the black dagger thrust upward into his brain.

She who called herself Blade withdrew the dagger, wiping it fastidiously on the cushion, then laying it on the floor. It shimmered, vanished.

A tall man, hairless, his naked skin blacker than night, stood beside Blade on the cushions.

"A fine gift," he said. "I really must thank you. Much more tasty than the soul of that Rivero fellow. He hardly had time to feel fear."

He reached into the cushions, drew out a small silk bag.

"And he had your payment ready, all along."

Blade took the pouch and tucked it into her sash. She picked up the black dagger from the floor of the room where she now stood alone, and sheathed it.

Her steps in the hallway, in the entry, on the street, were as silent as shadows in the moonlight.

ONE ════════

"Damn it, Doe, you should know better." Shadow slammed her goblet down so violently that some wine slopped over the edge. "You of all people should know better!"

"I didn't say *I* thought you took it," Donya said mildly. "I only said that's what it looked like. And of course it's all over town, you know, despite Lord Vikram's best efforts to keep it secret, so of course on top of stealing the ruby, he now thinks you're bragging it about Allanmere."

"Well, he should know better, too," Shadow grumbled. "Impotent old wretch, you'd think he'd have a bit of gratitude that I saved his worthless life last year, not to mention his place as the head of the Council of Churches."

"You know he won't admit it," Donya smiled. "He insists Bobrick was accidentally killed when the temple burned—which he also blames you for, by the way."

"Well, that *was* my fault—indirectly, anyway," Shadow chuckled. "At least he only had to rebuild the Temple of Urex. I had to rebuild a whole Guild, and he can be thanked for at least part of that. Anyway, that's kept me so busy I've hardly had time to hit the market these days, let alone pull off a complicated job like the Eye of Urex. Even if I'd been idiotic enough to do it."

"The plain fact is that *I* wouldn't have said anybody but you could have done it," Donya grimaced. "Since Vikram rebuilt the Temple of Urex he's paid heavily for extra protection, a lot of it magical, with you in mind, I think. *I* can't think of any way to have taken the Eye without your bracelet."

"Well, the simple fact is that I didn't," Shadow sighed. "Anyway, what would *I* do with the thing? I could hardly sell it around town, could I? Nobody'd dare to buy it, unless it was some squeaker looking to chirp to the guard and collect a reward, too. Besides, the thing's a fake."

"What?" Donya choked.

Shadow nodded.

"Uh-huh. Piece of glass. Good fake, very good; you have to know what you're doing and you have to get *close* to find out. That glow's from whatever magic is on it. Other than what the Temple of Urex might pay to get it back, it's worth no more than about five Suns for ornamental value except to the mage who cast it."

"That's impossible!"

"Doe, I know gems," Shadow said. "Have to, in my profession. Since the run-in with the Council, I've kept my eye on the Temple of Urex and Vikram."

"And on the Eye of Urex, supposedly the largest gem in Allanmere?" Donya asked wryly.

"What can I say?" Shadow said innocently. "Professional interest. Anyway, I've had people in the temple, and when I heard what some of them said, I went myself. Trust me, no self-respecting thief would have thought the Eye worth the bother, except maybe for ransom value. I don't know whether Vikram knows the Eye's a fake or not, but I do know he probably can't afford for his worshippers to find out, so he'd pay. Problem is, nobody's made a ransom demand. Frankly, I doubt that's what happened. Since it had to rebuild, the Temple of Urex just doesn't have enough money for a reasonable ransom. I should know."

"Vikram takes the theft as a challenge to the Council of Churches," Donya said dismally. "Of course, he's just looking for an excuse, you know, to strike at the Guild while it's still weak."

"And that's exactly why *I* wouldn't give him such an excuse," Shadow insisted. "But I may have an idea who did."

Donya leaned forward eagerly.

"Go on."

"Ever since I learned the Eye disappeared I've had feelers out," Shadow said. "I paid a pretty Sun or two in bribes, too, trying to trace the gem's history, see if there was anything there. I got a bite on that."

"Oh?"

"Turned out the Eye of Urex never had anything to do with Urex at all," Shadow told her. "That didn't surprise me after I found out the gem was a magicked fake. It used to belong to a mage named Baloran back before the Black Wars. Baloran, by the way, was a young mage brought south by Sharl III because of his talent for magical wards and protections. Seemed he was a rather paranoid fellow about thievery—Baloran, that is—and besides looking like a very valuable ruby the size of my fist, the Eye had its magical properties—Fortune alone knows what. Probably something obvious, given Baloran's reputation. Pretty little toy, eh?"

"Especially in a war," Donya nodded. "I read about Baloran in the histories. He was supposedly quite powerful at defensive magics and demon control, made several forays into the invading army himself, and supposedly managed to pick up quite a bit of foreign magic and treasure during the wars."

"Anyhow, the gem was stolen from Baloran not long after the wars, when he'd set up shop in Allanmere, at about the same time that the Guild started up," Shadow continued. "The timing of the two events may not be coincidental. Nearly a century later, by what chain of exchanges I can't

imagine, it ended up in the Temple of Urex under its first
High Priest, Solam the Blind, where it's been ever since. By
that time, though, Baloran had probably given up the gem as
lost; he'd left Allanmere right after the gem was taken and
set up his own enclave not far to the south, protected by
magical safeguards that were legendary. Later he moved
again, and this time no one really knows where.''

''Baloran wasn't elvan,'' Donya protested. ''I know that
from the histories. He would've been dead by then.''

Shadow shook her head.

''Rumor was that Baloran had learned a way to prolong
his own life,'' she said. ''One reason his defenses were so
good—everybody wanted his secret. Anyway, there are
records of transactions with him well over a century after he
arrived in Allanmere, too many records to doubt. There's a
number of mages in Allanmere who'll swear he's alive even
now.''

''And you think he took it?'' Donya asked skeptically.

Shadow shrugged.

''Whoever took it has to fit two requirements—a reason
to take it, and a way to take it,'' she said. ''As to physically
taking the gem, I'd have to agree with Vikram that it was all
but impossible. I know what kind of protections he had on
that thing. I could've done it, given enough planning, the
right equipment, and a little luck. Vikram, of course, had
access to it. Even his underlings didn't; since Bobrick tried
to have him killed, he's been more suspicious of his
assistants. The mage who casts the Temple of Urex's
protections has already testified under truthspell, and there
are no mages in Allanmere better at protective magic; that's
why Vikram hired him. Baloran, though, was better. I know
my own people, and none of them could've done it. And
there's no new talent in town; I watch sharp for that. So that
leaves only Baloran and Vikram who could've even gotten
their hands on the thing.

''Then there aren't many who'd have a reason,'' Shadow
continued. ''Stealing it for money—too naive; where'd you

sell it? Stealing it for ransom's foolish. Anyone who'd do that would have both the Guild and the Council of Churches on them at the first hint. Besides, the Temple of Urex can't pay, and anyone who'd done their research would know it. The only other value of the gem is its magic, and that's only valuable to the mage who created it. Baloran.''

"But *why*?" Donya asked. "You said yourself that Baloran probably gave up on the gem. Why would he take it, why now, and why frame the Guild in general or you in specific?"

"Framing me or the Guild keeps official attention on us, rather than looking for other suspects," Shadow mused. "That alone could be enough. As you've observed, I make a likely looking scapegoat. It could be that I'm the first thief Baloran thought capable of stealing the Eye, although from what I've heard of the previous Guildmasters, I don't know. Why he took it, and why now—now, that's what worries me."

Shadow sighed.

"It could be he simply wants or needs it back now for some reason. Maybe I'm seeing plots against the Guild behind every barrel. It could be that he only now located it because of the recent move of the Temple of Urex—the Eye being removed, however briefly, from its safeguards. Baloran wouldn't have had any opportunity to see it there unless he went there deliberately; he isn't a worshipper— no, don't ask me how I found that out. I *hope* there's some similar reason why now's the time. I hope I'm just being paranoid, because it looks to me like a ploy to set the Council of Churches against the Guild while it's still recovering from Ganrom's tenure as Guildmaster."

"But anybody might do that, including Vikram," Donya argued.

"You weren't listening, Doe," Shadow said patiently. "I already eliminated everyone who could have taken the gem. No matter who might *want* it taken, they still had to get it, or find someone who could. And that left only Baloran and

Vikram, remember, and Vikram's the *least* likely suspect. The Temple of Urex didn't need this little happening any more than the Guild does. Yes, it makes me look like the thief, but it also makes Vikram look like an incomparable bumbler. If Bobrick were still around I'd suspect him, but Vikram just isn't that devious. That leaves Baloran as the only person with a reason to take it, and, given his expertise on magical defenses, the ability to take it, and, as a bonus, the reasonable likelihood of getting away with it, too. He's hard to find, he's powerful, and I doubt if it matters much to him what disfavor he earns from anyone or any group in Allanmere.''

"Do you have any idea where Baloran is?" Donya asked.

"That's the bite I mentioned," Shadow said. "You know there's a few mages who traffic regularly with the Guild—"

"Yes, you've even corrupted my own mother on occasion," Donya said wryly.

"Anyway, I managed to gild the right palms," Shadow continued, "and learned that Baloran *is* still in the area, and that he's paid a few quiet visits to some of the local mages and suppliers over the years, and even more recently— recently meaning since I came to town. The Circle of Magi is quite curious about that—almost as much as I am, Baloran being something of a legend among mages—and there's been some speculation about where he's located. I've spent the three weeks since the Eye vanished ferreting out those speculations, and I've got a pretty good idea of the general area where he is, mostly by eliminating where he's *not*. It took every bit of the information chain I've put together since I gained the seat. I'm rather proud of it.''

"Then we should ride out in force and demand the Eye back," Donya stated. "I can get a good turnout of the City Guard for backing."

"No, no, that's exactly what I don't want to do," Shadow said hastily. "First of all, it puts you—and through you, the High Lord and Lady—in the position of backing the Guild openly against the Council of Churches. I don't think your

parents would agree to that, and worse, running to the law
for help would hurt my standing with the Guild, too. I really
don't want to go thundering off, leaving the Guild in
Aubry's hands. I can probably trust him, but why risk it?
Most of all, it tips our hand to Baloran. He could just vanish
again, you know, gem and all, and then we'd be no wiser as
to what he's up to. I'd prefer something more subtle—send
out a couple of spies, bribe a few mages to do some probing
about, if the Guild has to be involved at all.''

"But what makes you think the Council of Churches will
sit around and wait while you do that?'' Donya demanded.
"I don't think you realize just how hot Vikram is getting. If
what you say is true, he loses more face with every day that
gem's missing.''

"I'll talk to Vikram myself,'' Shadow shrugged. "Tell
him—under truthspell, if necessary—that I didn't steal it
and I'm on the track of the one who did.''

"Oh, Shady, he won't believe you no matter what,''
Donya said worriedly.

"I think he will,'' Shadow argued. "The Council's last
foray against the Guild cost them credibility with the City
Council. Vikram can't afford for that to happen again, so
he'll be hesitant to commit the temples at this point. If I can
convince him the Guild's not at fault—which I think I
can—he'll have a good excuse to wait without losing face.
I think he'll take it. I've already arranged to meet with him
in two days.''

"I don't agree,'' Donya said slowly, "but it's your
decision. What makes you think you can learn anything
about Baloran, anyway?''

"I came across some very interesting information about
Baloran in my investigations,'' Shadow smiled wisely. "If
I need it, I know someone who definitely knows quite a bit
about him.''

"Who?''

"No, no, can't reveal my sources,'' Shadow said quickly.

"I'd rather keep this one in reserve for an emergency, anyway."

"Well, at least give me a copy of what location you've got," Donya begged. "Mother's good at spotting; maybe she'll come up with something, and she's got contacts with more mages than you can probably bribe."

"That I can do," Shadow nodded. "I've marked the general area on a map, and I'll give you a copy to take back with you. Otherwise, though, just wait till I've had a chance to talk with Vikram before you take any action, will you?"

"All right," Donya said reluctantly. "But I wish you'd reconsider. Think about it, at least, will you do that?"

"Bet on it," Shadow said.

"High Priest Vikram's expecting me," Shadow said to the temple guards. "I'm a little early, maybe."

"No, the High Priest told us," the guard grinned. "Come on, we'll escort you."

Shadow followed the guards into the refurbished temple, eyeing the new ornaments and tapestries. Quite an effort for only a year and low funds!

The guards escorted her to a small room with only a table and two chairs and one door—the door they'd come in through.

"This can't be High Priest Vikram's meeting hall," Shadow said suspiciously. "What's going on?"

"This is a high-security matter, see?" the guard said patiently. "High Priest Vikram can't be seen consorting with the Guildmistress, can he?"

"We're not consorting, just talking," Shadow scowled. "When will I see him, anyway?"

"Soon enough," the guard said. "Now sit down and wait."

Shadow frowned but sat down, observing uneasily that two guards remained in the room with her while the others left, locking the door behind them.

Long minutes passed before the door opened; five more guards entered with a novice priest.

"That's her," the priest said, looking at Shadow. Without another word, he turned and left. One of the guards locked the door behind him.

"Now wait a minute—" Shadow began.

The guards were disinclined to wait.

"Well met, Guildmistress," Healer Auderic said as Shadow opened her eyes. "As I remember, we last encountered each other under similar circumstances."

"I hope this isn't going to become a habit," Shadow sighed. Her head ached wretchedly and her limbs were as stiff as if she'd lain there for days.

"Oh, Guild members are my best customers," Auderic smiled. "I really had expected to meet you again sooner, Guildmistress, after such a spectacular start."

"Well, Fortune favor me, you won't be seeing me again anytime soon," Shadow grumbled. "I wasn't made to lie around in a bed by myself."

Auderic chuckled and packed up the rest of his medical tools, handing Shadow a small vial.

"For pain, if your head or your cracked ribs give you any great difficulty," he told her. "They're all but mended, but bone-healing takes time. Take no more than two drops in a glass of wine. Send for me if you have any more problems."

Aubry entered as the healer left. He sat down on the edge of Shadow's bed and chuckled, eyeing her bandages.

"You've been very busy, I know"—he grinned—"but there's easier ways to find time for bed."

"And more interesting ways to play healer and patient," Shadow grimaced.

"*I'd* be interested in knowing," Aubry said, "what herd of wild horses stampeded over you and left you in a back alleyway of the market. Fortune's right hand was on you, no question, that it was one of Uncle's kids who found you, and that he went to Lady Donya and not some leftover loyalist of Bobrick's with a grudge.''

''Well, you very nearly answered your own question,'' Shadow grumbled. ''The Temple of Urex has a new cadre of ogres. I rather got the impression that Vikram didn't want to talk to me very much.''

''I don't agree,'' Aubry scowled. ''I read a very definite message, mostly written in black and blue. Maybe you should listen to it.''

''Ah, this is nothing,'' Shadow shrugged, wincing as she did so. ''But what did Donya say?''

Aubry shrugged.

''She'd been by looking for you,'' he said. ''Then she went to Uncle and his imps, had them looking. She came back later with you, called the healer, wrote you a note and left a packet, and then rode off right afterward like a dragon was on her heels.''

''I don't like the sound of that,'' Shadow frowned. ''Let's see the note and packet.''

The note was penned hastily in Donya's plain but neat script.

'' 'I've had three locators working on your map,' '' Shadow read. '' 'Plus Mother. They've pinpointed three possible locations within the area you showed me. One Mother located because what she calls the natural energies there have been interfered with. The other two, which are very close together, the locators chose because they were blind spots—spots where they couldn't sense anything at all. I'm betting on the easternmost spot. It's far enough from the forest that the elves wouldn't notice it, and it's on a rocky hill, easily defensible.

'' 'You just wouldn't listen, would you? I told you how upset Vikram was, but you just had to go, and alone! As I keep telling you, Shady, you're a rotten judge of human nature. So now we're going to do it my way.

'' 'I'm taking two squadrons of the guard as soon as I can get them provisioned and ready to go. This will save your reputation and mine. I really think this is a matter for the city anyway, and if this works out it'll satisfy the Council of Churches without the Guild ever being involved. I shouldn't be gone longer than a month or so.

" 'I'm returning your map, and I had copies made of what I could find in the histories about Baloran. In case there should be any problems—I don't expect so—the information may be useful. The ring in the packet isn't my signet—Father gave me a royal scolding for loaning it to you before—but it bears the Seal of Allanmere in case you need the City Guard to protect yourself.

" 'That's all for now. I've told Auderic to potion you so I can get a reasonable distance before you read this—' "

Shadow glanced up, comprehension dawning.

"Aubry! Just how long *was* I asleep?"

Aubry shrugged sheepishly.

"Five days. Auderic said your skull was cracked."

Shadow groaned.

"Five days! Fortune blight that healer. She must be leagues away by now, even with the guard to slow her down and maybe two days getting ready if she hurried—and she'd have hurried. I'll have to work fast."

"Work—what are you planning to do?" Aubry demanded. "Go running after her and leave the Guild at Vikram's mercy?"

"No," Shadow said. "I'm going to leave it at yours."

"That crack on your head addled your brains," Aubry said for the tenth time. "You can't leave me in charge of the Guild for a month, maybe more. There're thieves far more skilled than I. What if one of them challenges me?"

"They won't, because none of them wants the Guild in the mess it's in right now," Shadow said lightly. "Besides, I've been training you, and you're getting good with a knife. Keep Cris with you. If anybody bothers you, Cris can just burn the building down around all of you. That should scare them off."

"Shadow, that isn't funny!"

"Fortune favor me, it wasn't funny running through a burning temple with half my innards hanging out, either," Shadow laughed. "But it is now. Look at it this way, Aubry: you can't possibly do any worse as Guildmaster than Ganrom did, can you?"

"Well, look how *he* ended up," Aubry protested, but he was beginning to smile.

"Well, keep your fingers out of the Guild coffers or you'll end up the same," Shadow warned with a grin. "Prove yourself to me this time and I'll see about giving you some more responsibility in the Guild."

"I'd like to prove myself to you right now, before you leave," Aubry grinned back.

"That's tempting," Shadow smiled. "But I've got one last thing to do before I leave, and it may take some time."

"What's that?" Aubry asked.

Shadow glanced absently at the palm of her left hand.

"I've got to look up an old acquaintance."

TWO

"I've really gone to an amazing amount of trouble to find you," Shadow said conversationally, apparently not intimidated in the least. "Have some wine, won't you?"

Blade shook her head, her eyes narrowing.

"I remember you."

"You should." Shadow held up one slender hand, displaying a small, dagger-shaped black mark on her palm.

"Shadow," Blade nodded. "Guildmistress of the Guild of Thieves."

Shadow poured herself a goblet of wine, drank.

"You can see it's not poisoned," she said. "Really excellent wine."

Blade shook her head again.

Shadow chuckled.

"That's right, you drink Dragon's Blood. I suppose I owe the credit for the title as much to you as anybody. Your timing was impeccable, you know. I'd grown a bit weary of Bobrick's basement hostel, not to mention his entertainment. Did you see it, when I challenged Ganrom? Half dead on my feet, and I still took him out in proper style. Everyone was so impressed that I've had no challenges to speak of since I took the seat last year. And I got the credit for Bobrick, too—how anyone thought I had the chance, I don't

17

know. Thirty years of life is nothing to an elf. It was a good bargain.''

Blade gave the barest hint of a smile.

"Few are so pleased with the bargains they strike with me.''

"So I understand. I imagine that's what happened to Tomor on the Cloth Road, isn't it?''

Blade betrayed no reaction.

"What makes you think that?''

Shadow laughed softly.

"Oh, please. It's common knowledge that Rivero was about to put him out of business. Rivero turns up dead. Then Tomor turns up dead with your rather unmistakable mark on his hand. It wouldn't have been so obvious if either of them had been robbed, but not so much as a copper was disturbed although they were both wearing thousands of Suns in jewels. It isn't hard to guess that Tomor, having gotten what he wanted, probably balked at payment . . . or part of his payment, anyway. You're becoming quite a sore point with the law these days.''

"The same could be said of you, Guildmistress,'' Blade said softly.

"Only by the Council of Churches,'' Shadow chuckled. She quaffed the remainder of her wine and poured more. "The rest of Allanmere is very happy with me, you see. I've reformed the Guild considerably. Even the constabulary occasionally makes use of me and my contacts—not that you'd get them to admit it, of course. There's very little I don't know or can't find out. Although I will admit,'' she added, "that some information is hard to come by, such as how to find you. Few know, and fewer will talk.''

"Wise of them. I would be interested in knowing which one finally did.''

"I'm sure you would,'' Shadow grinned. "But as he'd probably like to keep his miserable life, I'll keep my peace.''

Blade's voice was expressionless.

"Nevertheless, he has taken a considerable risk—as have you, by coming here."

"And I'm about to add risk to risk," Shadow nodded. "You're not known for your restraint, but I'll ask you to hear me out before you decide to use that famous dagger of yours on me. You'll lose nothing by waiting, and I'll wager you stand to gain something. Will you listen?"

Blade paused, then nodded.

"Good." Shadow leaned her chair back, propping her feet up on Blade's table.

"As you've probably guessed, I'd like to hire you again. This time, however, I don't plan to pay you myself; I think you'll find the payment inherent in the task."

"I do not work that way," Blade said flatly.

"I know. Still, I don't think you'll find this too onerous." Shadow pulled a golden pin from the considerable ebony mass of coiled braids that crowned her head, using the pin to scratch one pointed ear. "A very large ruby which once adorned the Temple of Urex recently disappeared. A very professional-looking job, I'll admit, and done to look very much like my style. It was safeguarded well enough that people—some of them my own thieves, the sorry lot—are saying that no one but myself could've taken it. Nevertheless, I didn't take it, although the Council of Churches didn't seem to believe me when I told them so."

"Do you blame them?" Blade asked with the closest thing to a smile Shadow had yet seen on her face.

"What, you mean to say they might hold a grudge after I discredited them with the City Council, had their leader's assistant killed, burnt down their leader's temple, and unseated their toady from the Guild? Never." Shadow chuckled. Then she frowned and shook her head, rubbing it as if it ached.

"In any event," she said, more seriously, "they are rather upset. They've already made that displeasure rather tangible. I've spent a nasty year trying to turn that sorry excuse for a Guild into something the city can respect, but there's still a long and stony road ahead. I've worked too hard on the Guild to see it wrecked now in a conflict it can't possibly win. A few more years and I might've taken the risk.''

''So you wish the ruby found and returned?'' Blade scoffed. ''More your type of work than mine.''

''Not quite.'' Shadow sighed. ''I know where the ruby is; a mage has it. Obviously I want the ruby retrieved. I'd also like to find out why this mage wanted me blamed for the theft—a personal grudge against me, or against the Guild? And in either case, why this charade? Without knowing that, returning the ruby won't be enough; the mage will just try something more tricky. The obvious alternative is to have the ruby returned, and to have the mage become dead.''

Blade shrugged, idly turning the empty wine goblet in her hands.

''The problem is plain, the solution simple. I don't see why you think I would be willing to waive payment.''

Shadow eyed Blade curiously.

''The mage's name is Baloran.''

The goblet was suddenly stilled in the black-gloved hands. There was a long moment of silence, during which Blade gazed at the elf through eyes narrowed to mere slits.

''What is that to me?'' she asked at last.

Shadow folded her hands behind her head and smiled innocently.

''You're quite a mystery, Blade,'' she said. ''Nobody knows much about you, where you come from, even what you are. A year ago you piqued my curiosity. Three decades of one's life, after all, isn't a common price. You touched your lips to the palm of my hand and left a mark there that's roused my interest. Since then I've tried to see what I could learn about you and the strange dagger you bear, a dagger that leaves its victims not only dead but, according to the most powerful necromancers, devoid of their souls. There weren't many who knew anything about you, and fewer who would tell what they knew, but I did finally piece together a most interesting story.

"Apparently a powerful mage, named Baloran, famed for his power over demons and his remarkable longevity, once lived near Allanmere after the Black Wars. He wasn't much liked, for he was a nasty sort more suited to war than peace; and he wasn't much known, for he was quite a recluse. He was rumored to be immortal. He had a strong fear of thieves, that much is known, probably because he'd had something very valuable stolen in the past. Namely a large ruby which became known as the Eye of Urex. At any rate, he was very jealous of his possessions, and was known to set a great many safeguards on his valuables.

"Rumors of his wealth grew great, fueled by his heavy protections, and it was said that his keep held more wondrous secrets, taken during the wars, then the High Lord's own palace. Several thieves tried and failed to steal this treasure; most tried and died. But one escaped, nearly dead, murmuring of a wondrous dagger that held incredible power and the secret of eternal life.

"I can only speculate that this rumor fell upon a certain pair of ears and this person, Fortune alone knows how, penetrated Baloran's defenses and snatched the aforementioned dagger," Shadow continued. "A not-inconsiderable testimony to her ability. When this person gained the dagger, however, she learned that the dagger itself was merely another of Baloran's traps. True, it could bestow immortality; its owner—or prisoner—had the ability to drain life from others and into herself. And true, it bestowed great power upon the one who wielded it, for the dagger was in actuality the embodiment of a captive demon who was sworn to serve the wielder in all ways and feed on the souls of those the dagger slew.

"But there was a catch, for once the dagger was touched the owner could never be rid of it, and upon her death, the demon in the dagger would be freed and her own soul would go to replace it, to be freed in turn only when another poor dupe had been enslaved to the dagger and died."

Shadow took a deep breath and a swallow of wine.

"Actually, you can almost admire this fellow Baloran," she mused. "He must be incredibly clever to have pulled off this latest trick, and quite powerful to have come up with a binding like that dagger.

"Anyway, as a natural consequence, the new owner of the dagger took up as an assassin. This solved several problems: it let her accrue years of life by way of payment; it let her keep her demon dagger well fed and happy; it kept her comfortably wealthy; and it probably indulged a natural bloodthirstiness, to my way of thinking. Baloran left Allanmere for parts until now unknown, probably worried that the thief who stole the dagger could breach his defenses again in search of revenge.

"Well, tell me—how near right am I?" Shadow said at last.

"Very near to the truth," Blade said quietly. "And even nearer to death. I have killed many over the years for less knowledge than you have spoken in this room tonight."

Shadow raised an eyebrow but appeared otherwise unaffected by Blade's statement.

"You said you'd hear me out completely," she reminded Blade. "Haven't I made you the least bit curious?"

Blade's eyes narrowed thoughtfully.

"I am curious why you have placed yourself in a vulnerable position, meeting me in my own place alone and showing very dangerous knowledge."

Shadow shrugged. "Fortune hates a coward," she said. "Living safely is enough to kill by boredom alone. I said what I did because I'd like your help, and because you know I have nothing to gain now by lying to you, and also because I have a tempting bait to dangle before you—Baloran's present whereabouts."

"I am not easily manipulated," Blade said softly. "I could have such information from you quickly."

"I don't doubt that," Shadow said wryly, peeping over the table at the black dagger. "I wouldn't like to fall prey to your soul-sipping companion, and I doubt I'd like any other methods of persuasion you might offer. I'm sure you make Bobrick and his friends look like Ebraris's sweetest courtesans in that arena, by all accounts. However, I'm willing to give you the information you want without obligation on your part. Do what you like with Baloran; I don't care, especially if it puts him out of my misery. Doubtless he has numerous valuables that might interest you. Maybe you could persuade him to break the dagger's binding, if he could do it, which I don't know. At the very least you'd have revenge. All *I* want is the ruby, and I'm perfectly willing to share the risk in order to get it. That puts me under your watchful eye the whole time. But you really don't have to doubt my ability, or my willingness, to hold my peace about any information I've gathered about you. After all, we've had some profitable traffic, you and I. If word got about of any connection between us, I'd only stand to lose the confidence of my Guildmembers and the trust of people who don't know I traffic with assassins. And *that* is why I met you here, in your own place, alone—because I've also got something to lose by a little knowledge in the wrong place.''

Blade was silent a long moment, then nodded.

''I begin to see how you have held the seat,'' she said at last. ''For all your dangerous games, you have a shrewd mind.''

''Not really,'' Shadow chuckled. ''Just about five hundred years of experience in dealing with humans and the like. Mind, I'm not offering you a contract, or a bargain— I'm just pointing out that in this particular instance I think our interests coincide, and a—well—a partnership might be profitable on both sides.''

''And you only want this ruby, out of all Baloran's renowned riches?'' Blade smiled ironically. ''I find that difficult to believe.''

Shadow grinned shamelessly.

''Well, I can't go so far as to say that. But I won't begrudge you first choice. What you don't want might as well fall into my bag as sit and rot. I'd also like to know why this Baloran has such a lasting grudge against the Guild, and if others are involved. Otherwise, I'd merely like to see Baloran dead and the ruby returned. I wouldn't mind,'' she added thoughtfully, ''seeing Baloran die a particularly nasty death. This incident has been a real nuisance to me. Of course, I don't doubt that if you have your way, he'll die a nastier death than any I could imagine, anyway.''

Blade was silent for a moment.

''Tell me the rest,'' she said.

''Rest?'' Shadow raised her eyebrows.

''You have not told me all,'' Blade said coldly. ''Tell me the rest.''

Shadow grinned again.

''Very sharp. Yes, there is a rest. The fact is that the High Lord's daughter Donya—very much against my wishes—has taken two squadrons of the City Guard and taken to the road to where they think Baloran is. They've nearly four days lead. I want to arrive there before they do. You shouldn't mind that; Donya wouldn't take kindly to seeing anyone killed by an assassin, and she might very well kill him first.''

''What makes you think we can defeat a four-day lead?'' Blade asked neutrally.

''Donya's going to the wrong place,'' Shadow shrugged. ''She thinks like a warrior, not like Baloran would. She picked the most militarily likely location. Baloran wouldn't do that. He's devious and he knows the military—he was in the wars under Sharl III, remember. He relies on magical protections and invisibility, not physical defenses, and he isn't likely to have the troops for a military defense. The spot Donya picked is the last one he'd use—the logical place for someone to find him. I've got a better idea where to find him.

''Also, Donya took two squadrons of the guard. They'll have to go the long way, around the forest, because even the High Lord's daughter and Heir can't take fifty armed human soldiers through the Middle and Inner Zones of the Heartwood, and their numbers and hardware will slow them down. I know a much shorter way, a way good for two women alone without warhorses and armor. By the time Donya follows her false trail to its end and figures out what she did wrong, we should have at least a week's lead, maybe more.''

''I have no desire to encounter the High Lord's daughter and Heir,'' Blade said coldly. ''Much less two squadrons of the guard.''

''You think *I* do?'' Shadow demanded. ''Donya would skin me alive just for being there, much less anticipating and balking her. And I don't want her *or* the guard knowing that I'm working with you. I expect to get there, do what we have to do quickly and quietly, and get out of there before Donya and her friends ever arrive—and that's the way it had better work, for everybody's sake.''

Blade sat back silently in her chair, her eyes on Shadow. She pulled out the black dagger and began flipping it idly. Then her hand twitched slightly.

The dagger flew, whistling, through the air—

—to stick solidly into the table, less than a quarter inch from Shadow's hand.

Shadow smiled a little, her eyes never leaving Blade's. She made no move to touch the dagger.

Blade held out her hand.

''Blackfell,'' she said.

The dagger slid smoothly off the table and flipped into her hand. Blade chuckled.

''You are an elf to be reckoned with, Guildmistress Shadow. I will remember that. Very well, you have your bargain-that-is-not-a-bargain. You have a reputation for discretion. I like that. But you know that should word of me find its way past your lips, Blackfell will find you. You escaped me once; Fortune will not save you from me a second time.''

Shadow tilted her head in agreement.

"And you know that should word of our arrangements pass *your* lips, you might find yourself even more intimate with that dagger than you are already. But I think neither of us have anything to fear on that score."

Blade nodded, walked to a cabinet, and withdrew a small crystal flask of a liquid so dark purple that it was almost black, and two tiny crystal cups. She poured the dark liquid and offered one cup to Shadow.

"I do believe you owe me a round, at that," Shadow laughed. "But are you willing to carry me home after I collect?"

Blade smiled grimly and raised her cup. "To bargains," she said.

Shadow chuckled, raised her cup, and drank. Immediately she flushed dark red and coughed violently, knuckling tears from her eyes.

"Whoo. Whoo. To bargains, indeed!"

THREE ═══

As was typical in late spring in Allanmere, the Bright-water had overflowed its banks, and the flat swamp to the north was filled to capacity with water, muck, foul-smelling vapors, and equally foul-smelling inhabitants. Few cared, or dared, to follow the poor road that trod a narrow strip between the swamp's edge to the west and the fringes of the Heartwood to the east. Had there been travelers, they might have noted two women, one human and one elvan, and their mounts making their way cautiously along the slender trail. Had there been travelers, they might have noted that the human woman's steed, blacker than night, occasionally seemed to cast a misshapen shadow, and that the elf's horses shied nervously from it.

And then again, perhaps travelers would have noted nothing; for this was the easternmost edge of that swamp known as the Dim Reaches, famed for sights best left unremembered.

Although the darkness appeared to bother the women not at all, they camped soon after sundown, for Shadow's unhappy horses were starting to stumble over the treacher-ous way. The black horse vanished soon after, but not long after the woman managed to light a small fire, a black owl dropped into the camp, bearing a fat eel in its talons.

• • •

Donya reined in Ambaleis, only her warhorse's exquisite
reflexes preventing her from colliding with the rump of
Captain Oram's ugly buff gelding. Oram nodded mutely at
the horizon, where the sun was dipping over the edge of the
world.

"We must stop, my lady," he said apologetically. "The
men cannot continue at this pace."

Donya compressed her lips tightly, stifling her impa-
tience with difficulty. She was tired herself, and Ambaleis
was winded and sweating, but she would far rather have
pushed on for two more hours of riding time.

She looked behind her. The men were exhausted, hiding
it as best they could, but their mounts had no such pride.
The horses stood with their heads hanging down, foam-
lipped and panting. None bothered to crop the verdant grass
around them.

When Donya spoke, her voice was quiet.

"Set up camp, then. I will meet with you and your
lieutenants in my tent in an hour."

"Yes, my lady."

Donya dismounted and stepped toward her packhorse to
unload her tent, only to find two guardsmen there ahead of
her. They paused as they unloaded the tent, glancing at
Donya with faint surprise and reproach, then went about
their business.

"'My lady,' indeed," Donya growled to herself.

She turned back to her warhorse and reached for the
heavy cinches of the barding, only to be deprived of even
that task by one of the troop grooms. Donya gritted her
teeth and turned away, pulling at the fastenings of her
armor. One of the squires moved in her direction, but at a
fierce look from Donya wisely chose discretion over duty
and retreated.

"'My lady,' indeed," Donya repeated, scowling. "I
liked it better when it was just me and Shady, a campfire
and a pot of stew."

• • •

As Blade made no move to help with dinner, Shadow cleaned and skewered the eel, suspending it over the fire to cook, and sipped from a flask of wine uncomfortably in the silence as Blade stared unnervingly at her over the flames. How different from her travels years ago with Donya, where their camps were cozy fires, Donya's skillfully made lean-to shelters, and friendly evenings of stories, wine, and song! Shadow chuckled at the memory of Donya's diplomatically concealed disgust at her cooking; Shadow hoped Blade was more charitable or more inclined to cook, as her own skill in that area had not improved with the years.

"I was surprised when you agreed to this shortcut," Shadow said at last. "There aren't many who'll come through the Reaches when there's a good enough road through the forest, though it adds three days to a journey."

Blade shrugged. "Time is time," she said.

"But you seem well acquainted with the swamp," Shadow pried delicately. "One might speculate you've known it long."

Blade smiled thinly. "One might speculate whatever one likes."

Shadow sighed and slapped at mosquitoes. "And the insects don't appear to bother you, either."

Blade chuckled. "What would you give for such relief?"

Shadow grinned at the challenge. "The worth of a pint of blood, for that's what I've given this hour already to the denizens of this fair land, I'd swear." She pulled a small object out of her belt pouch, tossed it to Blade. "Will that suffice?"

Blade caught the tiny blue gem, eyed it critically for a moment, then tucked it into her belt pouch without speaking. She drew out the black dagger, then flipped it into the air directly over Shadow's head.

The dagger halted in midair as if it had struck something, spun like a top for a brief moment, then flew back to Blade's hand. Shadow felt a brief coolness, like the finest of mists, settle over her skin, and the whining attacks ceased immediately.

Shadow chuckled appreciatively. "Already your journey shows a profit for small labor." She diplomatically swallowed a jest that Blade might well hire out her services for control of vermin. "Would that the mage Baloran were as easily dealt with."

"He will be dealt with, easily or otherwise," Blade said flatly. She eyed the dagger considerably, then laid it down at her side. "Blackfell."

The dagger wavered, vanished. In its place sat the demon, naked and shining black in the firelight.

"Mistress."

Blade poked the eel with a stick, testing its doneness.

"Tell me, O demon mine, how greatly would you desire to drink the soul of Baloran who bound you?"

The demon trembled, its hands clenched tightly. "I would desire nothing more, save my freedom." It paused. "Perhaps not even that."

"And would you drink his soul slowly, savoring its agony?"

The demon's eyes glowed red. "Slowly."

Blade chuckled dryly. "You know that I seek him now, and that there is information I would have from him."

"I know it."

Blade swigged thoughtfully from her wineskin. "Should we succeed, I will have that information from him; gaining it will be enjoyable to me. After that he is yours as you wish."

The demon hissed softly. "You will succeed."

Blade resheathed the black dagger and looked across the fire at Shadow.

Shadow shook her head wonderingly. "I'll wager the unfortunate mage has nightmares about you," she said. "Many would think torture and death sufficient punishment."

"I am not many," Blade shrugged. "I have walked with my damnation by my side and met terms with it. Let him fear me if he is wise, and flee me if he is wiser still."

Shadow cut a piece of eel and said, "My conscience may forever belabor me for delivering him to you."

"Those foolish enough to heed such prickings deserve their pain." Blade cut a thick piece of eel and nibbled it indifferently, gazing out into the swamp mists. "You are a thief and should know that what a man cannot hold he should not dare call his in truth, be it soul or gold."

Shadow shrugged and said amiably, "I suppose it has a kind of justice to it."

Blade also shrugged. "I suppose, if that makes any difference. Will you play at ten-stone with me?"

Shadow raised an eyebrow dubiously, and said, "Well, but not for any stakes greater than money, if you please!"

Blade gazed back enigmatically and poured out a handful of small gems from her purse.

"For money, then."

Shadow raked up the last of the gems and dropped them into her pouch, eyeing her companion, half afraid that Blade would now fly into some violent rage.

Blade, however, only nodded. "And now your journey also shows a profit from small labor, and mine a loss from underestimating my opponent. A deadly flaw, that."

Shadow raised her wineskin in a toast. "And may such a flaw never cost you more than a few gems on the table."

Blade said nothing, only swallowed the last of the eel and turned away to her pallet. She thrust the black dagger into the earth beside her pallet and appeared to fall instantly asleep.

For Shadow, sleep came less easily. She sat staring into the fire, thoughtfully sipping her wine. At last she sighed, rolled herself up in her blanket, and finally slept.

● ● ●

It was not all bad. She had her own tent now, a cot instead of a hard pallet, warm furs instead of a tattered cloak, hot food instead of trail rations—or, worse, Shadow's cooking.

But, oh, she missed that tuneless voice, that impudent grin that never failed no matter how poor their rations or how foul the weather or her own temper.

She bent over the map, Oram moving to stand beside her.

"Six more days to pass the forest," Donya said thoughtfully. "If we can keep up the pace. Then—here, I think," she said, pointing to the nearer of the two spots she had marked.

"A good defensible location," Oram agreed, beckoning his two lieutenants forward. "I don't know this land, though. Is this all flat plains?"

"As best we know," Donya shrugged. "The land's too remote from Allanmere to be used by the farmers or herders, and too far from the Sun Road to be of interest to travelers. It's never been mapped in any detail, except for the general features marked here. Chart it yourself, if you like, and make a few Suns from the Mapmakers' Guild."

"Two days, then, to reach the place," Oram said thoughtfully. "But best to make an early stop and arrive on the morning after. If there is—conflict, best the men are rested, fed, and ready to fight."

"Mmmm," Donya agreed reluctantly. "All right. But there'd better not be fighting. Remember, we're speaking of Baloran, the mage who did more damage to the barbarian horde than Allanmere's army. You and your men are here to make a good show, not to throw your lives away so the Council of Churches can have its bauble back."

"The Council of Churches might not agree with your priorities, my lady," Oram chuckled.

"Doubtless they won't," Donya said, rolling up the map. "But I'm not concerned with pacifying them. I'm only concerned with averting a large-scale conflict in the city, and if they don't like the way I deal with it, Vikram can take his grievances to Baloran himself. Better that than—"

"Than to Guildmistress Shadow?" Oram suggested kindly.

"Yes." Donya sighed. "Shady's my friend, and of course I don't want to see her hurt, Oram, but there's more to it than that. The Guild is becoming an elvan voice again, and we need that liaison with the forest elves. And we need the Guild itself as a kind of control on thievery in Allanmere. We can't afford the kind of chaos that was emerging under Ganrom. Shady's the one to keep her people in order, however much she hates the job, and I'm going to do everything I can to see that she's there in that seat with the power to do it."

Shadow awoke to the smell of roasting meat. To her amazement, two marshconies and a large serpent were spitted over the fire and nearly done. Blade was still asleep; however, at the first rustle of movement from Shadow, she jolted upright, dagger in her hand.

"It seems your companion hunted well last night," Shadow commented uneasily.

Blade stretched sinuously. "Well, better than preserved trail food. And for my stomach's sake, better him cooking it than you."

Shadow wrinkled her nose, ignoring the barb. "Fine, but you can have the serpent. I don't like snakes."

Blade raised an eyebrow. "You ate the eel."

"Eels aren't snakes."

Blade shrugged indifferently. "Meat is meat."

Blade's statement conjured up an unpleasant curiosity, which Shadow stifled for the sake of her appetite. She ate the better part of one of the marshconies with tough trail biscuits.

Around midday, a heavy, drenching rain began to fall, and both women retreated to the depths of their cloaks. By late afternoon, the swamp had risen and begun to lap at the edges of the trail, and even Blade's mount was finding the footing slippery and treacherous, while Shadow's roan and bay were sliding helplessly.

"We'd better find higher ground and stop," Shadow called ahead.

"An old trail shelter lies but two miles ahead," Blade shouted back. "We can make it that far."

"Then stop for a moment," Shadow called. "I've got to scrape my horses' hooves or we're both going into the swamp."

Blade stopped and sat impatiently while Shadow scraped a thick caking of slippery mud from her horses' hooves while the patient beasts shivered and snorted wearily. The swamp mud was heavy and almost as slick as soap, and by the time she had finished, Shadow herself was liberally smeared. Grimacing, she stepped over to a nearby pool to rinse off the worst of her burden.

She had barely squatted beside the water when something— a long, scaly, foul-smelling something—emerged from the pool and wrapped itself firmly around her waist. Shadow had just enough time to reflexively reach for her dagger and gulp a last breath before a tremendous jerk toppled her into the stinking muck.

Shadow cut desperately at the tentacle around her waist, horrified to feel others loop around her legs. Her sharp knife barely penetrated the scaled surface, and she felt herself being pulled deeper. She cut through the tentacle at last, only to feel another wrap firmly around her straining chest. She dimly noticed a brief agitation in the water above her.

Suddenly there was another dagger in her hand, a dagger that felt icy cold even considering the chill water. Shadow flailed wildly with it, her lungs aching, and felt it cut through the clasping tentacles like a sword through butter. The last tentacle squeezed convulsively around her chest, forcing the air out of her lungs, then released her. Shadow flailed awkwardly to the surface and crawled into the shallows, collapsing into the mud as soon as she was clear of the pool.

"Blackfell," Blade's voice said, and the cold dagger disappeared from her hand. A black-gloved hand, extended, appeared in Shadow's field of vision.

Panting, Shadow took the hand, which pulled her upright with remarkable strength. Shadow knuckled mud out of her eyes to meet Blade's rather amused expression.

"It is best to avoid deep pools," she said. "Fell-beasts often live therein."

Shadow gasped out a chuckle, gesturing at the many pools surrounding them, any of which, to appearances, could be a well or a puddle.

"And how," she wheezed, "do you tell the deep ones?"

"By falling in," Blade said amusedly. "Shall we continue?"

"Fortune favor me," Shadow gasped, "as quickly as we can, please!"

To Shadow's humiliation, she was too exhausted to make the climb to the horse's back and had to accept a hand up from Blade; once mounted, she could do little but slump over the horse's back, weakly scraping at the mud caking her.

Donya stared moodily out the flap of her tent and sighed. The rain was pouring down in sheets. The men were sharing their tents so that some could be converted to roofs to shelter a few pitiful fires. The men huddled around these fires, sharing wine and stories and what cheer they could muster.

Donya ached for such company, but she made no move to join the men. She'd already tried once, blithely stepping to one of the nightly fires. The jocund conversation had ceased abruptly, an awkward silence descending. They did not mean to exclude her, but any conversation quickly palled, and Donya's few bawdy jokes, told in the hope of making the men more comfortable, only elicited brief and embarrassed glances. Finally she'd stopped trying. The men deserved what enjoyment they could get on this miserable journey.

"Ah, Shady, you're the lucky one," Donya murmured. "Likely you're half-drunk by now, in a soft bed with some lusty fellow. When will I ever learn?"

The trail shelter was, indeed, exactly where indicated. It was old and very weathered, but appeared sturdy and had been built on a rise above the flood level. Shadow fed and stabled the miserable roan and bay in the attached lean-to, where only a little rain was dripping in, then returned to the main shelter. Blade had already started a cheery fire, and more dry wood was stacked in a corner.

Shadow saw the empty sheath at Blade's hip and looked around dubiously. "Where's your—ah—companion?"

"Hunting."

"Good." Shadow grinned. "I'm eager for hot food this night." She shrugged out of her sodden cloak. "I'd wager I've brought in enough water to fill a good tub."

Her pack, unfortunately, was nearly as soaked as the cloak. Shadow looked uncertainly at the door, then she sighed and stripped, wrapping herself hurriedly in her one nearly dry blanket.

Blade glanced at her dispassionately. "What if an enemy came upon us in the night?"

"In this?" Shadow chuckled. "Any who might brave this rain deserves whatever joy the sight of my body would give him. Your familiar stands a fine guard against anyone fool enough to attack you, but I'd say even he can't fend off choking sickness." She spread her wet clothes near the fire.

To Shadow's surprise, Blade hesitated, then nodded, but took her blanket into the lean-to to change. Shadow had to chuckle at this uncharacteristic modesty. Did Blade think she was a lover of women, and one foolish enough to leap heedlessly upon so dangerous a playmate? Humans and their strange body-shyness! Then she diplomatically stifled her amusement as Blade returned, although she had to bite her lip to keep silent when she noticed that her companion had retained her boots and gloves, and the blanket was so swathed and pinned about her as to leave hardly a fingers-breadth of skin showing.

Shortly after Blade came back, Blackfell returned in his human shape and dropped two large fish at the hearth. Blade replaced the dagger in its sheath, looked pointedly from the fish to Shadow, and walked over to sit at the other side of the hearth.

Shadow irritatedly cleaned and boned the fish, then simmered them with her carefully hoarded wine and vegetables in the pot to make a stew. When Blade approached, Shadow bit back a dry comment about help arriving better late than not at all, but Blade merely produced a plain brown stone tied to a thong, and tied the thong to the pothook, suspending the stone in the soup.

"Soupstone?" Shadow asked curiously. "It's been a bit since I've seen one. I had one once, been in my family for centuries." She grimaced. "A couple of loyal friends permanently borrowed it just before I came to Allanmere. Where did you get one?"

"From an overcurious fool who no longer needs it," Blade said idly.

"I take it your demon's a magic-sniffer, then," Shadow said. "Soupstones are subtle magic."

"Stronger than that on your bow," Blade shrugged.

Shadow grinned and carefully unwrapped the oiled leather protecting the unstrung weapon. Its dark wood was finely carved in intricate vine and flower designs, and polished to a high gloss.

"There's no magic in this, just a simple keep-spell," Shadow said. "I carved it myself over four hundred years ago. A—friend, if you will, in the forest was keeping it for me. It seemed to belong there better than wandering the world with me."

"I wonder that you risk it on this journey."

Shadow shrugged.

"I've regretted leaving it behind," she said. "A good weapon which saves me but once has earned its worth. Why trust my life to less?"

"I will toss you daggers for it."

"I'm glad you so appreciate my workmanship"—Shadow chuckled—"but this bow is one I'd as soon keep, at least until the risk of this trip is behind me. Besides, this one would be far too short and flimsy for you. However, I'll offer this: I'll gladly carve you another as fine, but made to your grip and pull. Will that suffice?"

Blade nodded.

"And what will you take as your prize, should you win?"

"One of your flasks of Dragon's Blood. I saw you had many, Fortune alone knows how."

This time Blade laughed, rather coldly. "I see you are growing to share my addiction," she said. "Beware, elf, for such a habit is costly to feed." She picked up a half-charred stick from the fire and drew two targets on the wall. "Three daggers each?"

Shadow nodded and drew her three, flipping each for balance, then let fly, only a little hampered by the necessity of clutching her blanket as she threw. Blade's three daggers flew with equal swiftness to their target.

Silently the two women examined their own targets, then each other's.

Shadow shrugged. "I see them the same," she said.

Blade's eyes narrowed. "As do I. Another toss?"

"All right. Off hand this time?"

"Yes."

Thunk. Thunk. Thunk.

This time, on examining the targets, it was Blade who chuckled. "You failed to tell me you were two-handed."

"As did you," Shadow retorted with a grin. "Well, what will it be this time? Blindfolded or standing on our heads?"

Blade smiled dryly. "I need no further proof that we are matched too evenly to win by anything but chance, and I fear you are the favored in that arena. I will pay my forfeit if you pay yours."

"All right," Shadow agreed cheerfully. "But in all honesty I'll say that your flask of Dragon's Blood is more valuable than any bow I could make, I'm afraid."

"A flask of Dragon's Blood is soon gone," Blade said negligently. "A fine weapon is worth keeping."

Shadow smiled at the compliment.

"I'll choose the wood as soon as we reach the forest— tomorrow, if the rain allows."

"I will pay my forfeit in advance, then," Blade said, "as it will be welcome after our stew—for which I have a great appetite now."

The stewed fish was as delicious as Shadow could have hoped, and the tiny sip of Dragon's Blood she allowed herself drove the last remnants of cold from her body; however, the warmth, full stomach, and potent liquor conspired to make her so sleepy that she soon sought her pallet, leaving Blade to look over their map.

Sometime during the night, Shadow awoke to a strange cry. The shelter was only dimly lit by the red embers of the dying fire, but Shadow's hands had unerringly drawn the dagger from its hiding place under her pillow. She was half out of her pallet before she realized that the cry had come from Blade's pallet in the far corner, and that Blade was not alone there. Faint firelight shimmered off smooth black skin.

Slowly, Shadow replaced her dagger and slid back under the covers, shivering as the cry came again. She couldn't tell if it was a cry of pleasure or pain.

It was some time before she slept again.

The rain had stopped in the morning, but the trail was so soggy that despite her hurry Shadow had some doubts about attempting travel. Blade, however, insisted on pressing onward as the forest edge was no more than half a day's ride ahead, and Shadow reluctantly agreed.

Shadow's fears came to nothing; they reached the forest edge with no mishap, although the poor roan was sweating and blowing from its struggle with the sucking mud of the swamp. Shadow pulled up to change horses and to consult her map.

Blade reined in beside her. "What path have you planned? We cannot rejoin the Sun Road from these parts."

Shadow shook her head. "No. There's a trade road to the north that runs east through the Middle Zone of the forest and later the Inner Zone. We'll take that."

Blade raised one slender black eyebrow. "You think we can avoid the elvan patrols?"

Shadow grinned and touched the thick coil of her braided black hair.

"Technically, I'm old enough for Matriarch status. It's not a title I use often, but with me escorting you we shouldn't be challenged more than once or twice. Word gets around."

"Blackfell cannot hunt in the Middle Zone, not by the Compact."

"I can, and light a fire as well," Shadow said. "But it might be best if you kept yourself . . . inconspicuous. Our welcome might be cold if the patrols learned the identity of my guest. Guests."

"I dislike traveling under elvan sufferance," Blade frowned ominously.

Shadow shrugged. "There's not much choice. The only road around the Inner Zone is the Sun Road itself, and it takes us days too far east—and, of course, that's the way Donya and her guards are going, so we'd lose our lead. As you say, time is time. I'm not unacquainted with the elves in these parts."

"We can continue through the swamp. I know a short road, even shorter than your route through the Inner Zone," Blade argued.

Shadow looked dubiously at Blade. "I'd rather not," she said. "You're talking about the worst part of the Reaches, and the trail's bad enough now. I'm not sure my horses can make it."

"As you say, then," Blade said at last. "I cannot be sure the swamp road is still good in any wise."

They turned the horses north and found that the overland way was densely overgrown and slow going. It was late afternoon when they finally reached the trade road, and Shadow, tired and well scratched by briars, suggested they stop and make camp. Blade scowled but agreed.

As soon as they camped, Shadow disappeared into the forest, to reemerge nearly an hour later with a stout length of ash wood and two dead rabbits.

"Here's dinner and the beginning of your bow," she told Blade. "I'll take your measure tonight, but it'll be some time before it's done, I'm afraid."

"I feel eyes upon me," Blade said suspiciously.

"I don't doubt it," Shadow said cheerfully. "You never see an elvan patrol until they want you to, and elves have other eyes that go on four feet or on wings. Doubtless we'll meet a patrol at some time or another. I suppose I'd better start doing my hunting on the hoof, else you might be challenged while I'm gone. Well, I'll start a fire and we'll try the tenderness of these rabbits. I found some roots and berries that should go well with them."

"All that in an hour?" Blade asked skeptically.

"Ah, but we're in *my* land now," Shadow said contentedly. "I'd missed it more than I thought."

"Yet you live in the city by choice."

Shadow chuckled. "It's said among the elves that a baby's world is small, only a few feet across. Yet as the child's spirit grows, so too does his world—larger and larger, until one day it grows as big as the forest, and, for some, even beyond that. I suppose you could say my spirit grew until the forest wasn't big enough to hold it. Now I'm working on a spirit-holder the size of a city."

Blade glanced at her over the rim of her cup. "And when your spirit grows too big for the world?"

"Why, then it's time to die so my spirit can find a bigger one to grow into," Shadow laughed. Then she sobered. "I suppose it's no joke for you. I've heard it said among humans that elves live with their heads so high in the treetops that they often tread heedlessly on others."

Blade shrugged. "Those who walk bare-flanked through the forest need expect no pity from the thorns. The wise put leather and cloth between their skin and that which pricks it."

Shadow ruefully surveyed her scratched skin. "Yet it seems some thorns are mightier than any cloth and leather."

"That comes of wishing the convenience of a horse's back. When you ride, you place yourself somewhat at the mercy of your animal. I am favored," Blade said cynically, "in that my mount, unlike yours, considers only my skin in its choice of path. Give me those rabbits before you ruin them. Your culinary skill will doubtless shorten my life and therefore lengthen Baloran's."

Shadow diplomatically refrained from a return barb on the comparison of Blade's payment and her own for the convenience of a mount; instead she fell to work on the bow, carving away excess wood to rough out the initial form. At last she pulled out a length of cord and motioned Blade to stand.

"I'm measuring you for length and pull of your bow," Shadow explained as she applied the cord. "The bow should be the length from shoulder to knee."

"That seems long."

"It is. But the bow will be shorter when it's bent," Shadow told her. "Too small a bow won't let you put strength behind your arrow. Make a hard fist and bend your arm."

Blade complied, and Shadow felt the muscles of Blade's upper arm, forearm, and wrist. Blade appeared markedly uneasy under the examination, pulling away from Shadow as soon as Shadow came too near her gloved hands, but made no explanation.

"Men's bows are easier to make than for a woman," Shadow said placatingly. "It's easy to see a man's muscles and judge their pull, but women often have strength without visible muscle. I can tell you're stronger than you look."

Blade raised one eyebrow. "I have been underestimated on occasion."

"Men, especially humans, tend to underestimate women as they're used to judging each other by height and bulk, even if they don't know it," Shadow agreed. "Often they forget the advantages bought by speed, skill, and a cool head over sheer force and strength."

Blade sat back to watch Shadow work on the bow. "I had the impression you seldom fought."

Shadow grinned. "I avoid a fight in earnest when I can, as I've enjoyed my long life and would as soon it continued. But as anyone at the Guild will say, I enjoy a good practice bout as well as the next. For every burly man I best on the floor, there are three watching who will decide not to cross me, after all."

"And what if one beats you?"

Shadow shrugged. "I'll worry about that when it happens. Most human men are all strength and no wit, good enough in the bedsheets but easy prey in a fight."

"But there are elvan men as well."

Shadow put down the bow to take a piece of rabbit.

"Elvan men don't fight me. Those younger than I respect a Matriarch's right to lead. Those older see no need to compete. Oh, one day someone—man or woman, elf or human—will see me bested. Bet on it. And someday, should I idiotically choose to remain Guildmistress that long, I'll taste secret death in the night when someone more clever than myself hungers for the seat. But I'll not let the fear of tomorrow spoil the joy of today."

Blade chuckled contemptuously. "I do not find today as joyful as all that."

"Then you need a touch of the Mother Forest in you, as we used to say," Shadow laughed. "There's much to be joyful for. I live. I'm a free woman in fine health—give or take a few remaining bruises—and an elf in the green forest. I have money at my belt and more behind me. I have fresh meat on the stick and fine liquor to drink with it. The breeze is sweet with forest scents and my horse is a fine beast. Best of all I'm out of that malodorous swamp. Aren't these reasons to be joyful?"

"If you want nothing more than the moment, like the beasts in the forests," Blade taunted.

"I *am* a beast in the forest," Shadow grinned. "And certainly I want more. I want a soft bed and a man in it, I want a certain mage dead, I want to follow the sun to the ends of the world. But those will come or not, as Fortune wills, so I'll enjoy what I have and not worry over what I don't."

"If you want a man—" Blade shrugged.

"That can wait," Shadow said quickly, unable to repress a small shudder.

Blade saw the shudder and smiled coldly. She wiped rabbit grease from her chin and was silent.

"On this road, our travel should be faster," Shadow said to change the subject. "We'll reach the Middle Zone by sunset tomorrow, with steady riding."

"How will we know?" Blade asked. "Forest is forest to me."

Shadow looked at her curiously. "Strange for one so familiar with the swamp to say that. On a road like this there'll be patrols to meet us. In less-traveled areas, there are magical symbols placed on rocks and trees at intervals to warn off unescorted humans. The Compact tells all that."

Blade rolled her eyes. "As I said, I dislike traveling under elvan sufferance. I never became acquainted with such details."

"It's the law that all humans learn the Compact and its terms."

"What care I—" Blade abruptly fell silent, scowling around her into the darkness.

"Perhaps I will review its terms," she said through gritted teeth, "when we return to Allanmere."

Shadow laughed, earning her an even blacker scowl from Blade.

"If any elves hear you, which I doubt at the moment, they don't care which laws of Allanmere you keep or ignore. They care only that you respect *their* law while in their place."

"Sensible of them," Blade said icily, flinging down the last of her rabbit. She strode to her sleeping pallet and pulled the covers over her.

Shadow chuckled to herself and picked up the bow, resuming her careful carving.

In the morning, Shadow and Blade breakfasted on fresh berries and cold rabbit, then hurried on. The trade road, though nothing more than a well-worn trail, made travel both quicker and easier. The increased speed of their travel raised Shadow's spirits, and she sang bawdy elvan ditties until Blade suggested that relief from Shadow's tuneless warbling might well be worth the trouble of slitting her throat.

Shadow managed to shoot a few small game birds from horseback for the evening, but they lunched on horseback, wishing to make the zone borders before they camped. It was, in fact, late afternoon when Shadow pointed out a large boulder at the side of the road, engraved with a strange symbol.

"There's the first Middle Zone marker," she said. "It's actually another two miles ride before we reach the true zone border."

"A warning to humans might be better written in the human tongue," Blade said sarcastically. " 'Return, lest danger be thy part' in elvan symbols means little to most of humankind.''

Shadow looked sharply at Blade but said only, ''Humans aren't expected to translate them; they're just markers.''

As they road, they passed a second marker, then a third. Suddenly, without warning, they were surrounded by five leather-clad elves, two with bows at the ready.

''Fair evening, kinsmen,'' Shadow said cheerfully, giving a warning shake of her head at Blade, who had drawn two daggers. ''There's game enough in the woods that you needn't point your arrows at such a scrawny bird as myself.''

A male elf, who appeared to be the leader of the group, nodded, and the bows were lowered.

''Pardon, kinswoman,'' he said politely. ''Your name and business, and that of your companion, in the Middle Zone?''

Shadow slid off her horse.

''I'm called Shadow, and my companion and I only pass through on our way north.''

''You give no name for the human.''

Shadow shrugged.

''Her name isn't mine to give or keep. She travels under my protection, under the terms of the Compact.''

''Why, I know the Matriarch Shadow,'' a slender female elf said. ''She's the very Guildmistress of the Guild of Thieves in Allanmere!''

The leader smiled and clasped Shadow's hand.

''Doubly welcome, then, Matriarch—and you also, nameless human woman! It's almost nightfall, and our patrol duty ends at sundown. We have meat and wine, and dreamweed to smoke with it—will you share food and fire?''

Shadow hesitated. The insult of refusing food and fire was unthinkable, but Blade was a chancy one to put at such a gathering.

''Of course, we are honored to share food and fire,''

Blade said suddenly. She smiled slowly. "And my lady's kinsfolk may call me—Amber."

"Well met, Amber," the male elf grinned. "I am Laurel. I make known to you my mate, Teria, and our friends Sereth, Melana, and Willow. Come, Matriarch," he said, noting Shadow's hesitation, "don't let it be said that a human came more eagerly to elvan hospitality than our own kin."

"Of course, Laurel," Shadow said quickly. Inwardly, however, she frowned, wondering what game Blade was playing.

The patrol was camped only a mile farther north, at a cleared area at the side of the road. Shadow's birds were quickly cleaned and added to a plump side of boar roasting over the fire.

While the meat cooked, Teria poured wooden mugs of moondrop wine, and Willow lit pipes of dreamweed.

"Strange goings-on these days," Laurel mused, accepting a goblet and pipe. "Merchants skirt Allanmere like a robbers' den and rumors of conflict come even to the inner reaches of the Heartwood. None of us go often to the city—will you give us news of how the Guild fares?"

Shadow drew deeply on her pipe, enjoying the familiar bite of good dreamweed in her throat, to be allayed by the potent wine.

"The Council of Churches has a flea up its bottom," she shrugged. "They're missing a gem and so assume that I took it. They've gone so far as to make baseless threats— maybe a little more than threats," she admitted under Teria's dubious look.

"Others take such threats more seriously," Melana said, her voice soft and musical. "Many of our kin who go to the city have joined the Guild now that it again welcomes us. How will the Guild fare if the Council makes good its threats?"

Shadow shook her head. "It won't come to a conflict like

it did before. If necessary I'll swear the Guild's innocence before the City Council under truthspell. I don't want to do that; it makes me look weak and the Guild vulnerable, that the Council of Churches can put that kind of pressure on me. But I don't think it'll come to that. Even now Amber and I journey to consult a powerful seer in the north on this concern.''

"Do you carve a spare bow for yourself?" Willow asked, gazing at the piece of wood on which Shadow was working.

"Ah, no. This is for Amber, won fairly in a game," Shadow said, diplomatically not mentioning the forfeit Blade had paid.

Teria smiled at Blade. "Then you excel at games of chance?"

Blade had refused the wine, but drew deeply on her pipe.

"I have been known to win a copper or two at ten-stone."

"Then we must try her skill," Laurel chuckled. "But you should be more moderate with that dreamweed, lest we win more than a copper or two from you. That is not the lesser dreamweed we commonly sell to the city, and humans often find its effects overpowering."

"I thank you for your warning," Blade said thinly, taking another deep puff on the pipe. She drew up a ten-stone grid on the ground. "And I would likewise thank you for a refill of my pipe."

The other elves gathered around the grid, and Willow glanced questioningly at Shadow.

"Thank you, but no," Shadow laughed, bending to her carving. "This sheep has no desire to be fleeced tonight."

Hours later, Teria walked over to Shadow, staggering a little.

"Fleeced, indeed," she muttered. "Your friend is an expert shearer." She plopped down beside Shadow. "Is there any wine left?"

Shadow chuckled and found a skin still half-full, then watched as the elf downed most of it at one gulp, spilling quite a bit on herself in the process.

"My mate," Teria grumbled, "has already lost a week's patrol fees, and has he his way he'll lose another. He's kept a sober head, though, which is more than I can claim. Your friend has a remarkable head for dreamweed and I foolishly tried to match it." She slapped Shadow amiably on the shoulder. "Borrow him this night if you like, for I know my fuzzy head will be long asleep by the time he seeks our pallet." Teria tipped the last of the wine into her mouth, then staggered off to her pallet, laughing to herself.

Gradually, the other elves surrendered the game to Blade, whose pouch, at final accounting, was considerably heavier. As the elves finished the last wine in the skins and sought their pallets, Laurel glanced at Shadow and grinned, raising one eyebrow questioningly. Shadow grinned back and nodded, and Laurel snatched the last full wineskin before Willow could, bringing it with him.

"You will pardon Sereth and Willow, that neither of them offered you companionship," Laurel apologized. "But Melana is ripening and unlike myself, Sereth and Willow may have living seed. Melana's ripening surprised us, and we were preparing to return to the tribe when we met you."

"Perhaps Amber and I can accompany you," Shadow suggested. "We aren't going to the center, but we could go as far as Crescent Pool before we turn north."

Laurel frowned briefly, and he gave Shadow a vaguely embarrassed look.

"Forgive my discourtesy, kinswoman," he said at last. "But I must ask that you do not enter the Inner Zone with—Amber."

"Oh?" Shadow spoke quietly, but she was shocked. For a Matriarch and any guest she escorted to be refused entry to the Inner Zone was highly unusual, if not unthinkable.

Laurel glanced at Blade uneasily.

"The others are young," he said. "They do not know who it is riding at your side. I will say nothing, for you are a Matriarch and what games you play, however dangerous, you must play for a reason. But neither can I allow that creature into the heart of our land. I pray that you understand and forgive me.''

Shadow sighed and nodded.

"I understand," she said. "No offense taken, Laurel. We'll ride back west tomorrow."

"Through the Reaches?" Laurel asked, his eyes widening. "Can you not skirt the Inner Zone and continue north? It would be at least somewhat shorter than the Reaches."

"There's no road around the Inner Zone, and we can't make a good pace through the underbrush with the horses," Shadow said regretfully. "We can't spare the time; I really can't explain."

"Now I regret my refusal," Laurel murmured. "The Brightwater has doubtless flooded the Reaches, and there are rumors of ill happenings at such times. Perhaps, after all—"

"No, I can't blame you for your caution," Shadow sighed. "Knowing—well—Amber, I can't say I'd have decided any different in your place. I'm not that comfortable with her motives myself. I don't think I'd have brought her into the Heartwood at all if—well—if matters weren't so urgent."

"I am sure"—Laurel chuckled—"given the identity of your companion, that were matters not urgent you would scarcely have brought her at all."

"That's true," Shadow laughed softly, glancing at Blade to make sure she hadn't heard. "But I'll tell you this— nothing's so urgent that I want to spend the rest of the night talking about it! I hope some of that wine's for me?"

"Indeed it is," Laurel smiled, opening the skin and handing it to Shadow.

"Wonderful," Shadow sighed after her first hearty gulp. "Ah, nothing like home brewing. And now"—she grinned wickedly—"what other traditional amenities can I expect?"

"Why, Matriarch," Laurel said innocently, "if I failed to offer you all the comforts of home, what kind of kinsman would I be?"

"That"—Shadow smiled—"is just what I'd like to find out."

FOUR ≡

"Well, that was a pleasant change," Shadow sighed, patting the three wineskins Laurel had given her contentedly. "At least for me. I can't imagine, though, why you wanted to stop."

Blade had ridden silently for some time. At last she spoke.

"You had won most of my gems," she shrugged. "I saw a chance to replace them."

For a moment Shadow wondered uneasily if Blade had some method of cheating, and if so, why had she not used it when gambling with Shadow herself? Then another thought crossed her mind.

"That wasn't *all* your money, was it?" Shadow asked amazedly. "You have more back in Allanmere, don't you?"

Blade shrugged. "What should I do with it?" she asked. "I have no permanent rooms, and those I rent are in areas in which I could not safely leave money. My needs are few and those are fulfilled by one means or another. I never keep more money than I can easily carry. I will know in the future, however, not to match my luck against yours!"

Shadow was stunned to silence at the thought that an assassin of Blade's caliber might own no more than a pouch of gems. But then, as Blade had said, Dragon's Blood was indeed an expensive addiction!

"I had thought we would ride north," Blade said at last. "Yet you have turned us nearly back upon our track."

"Yes. Well—I decided we'd take your swamp road," Shadow said awkwardly. "It would be hard for me to pass through the Inner Zone without being obliged to stop and visit, and—"

"What you mean," Blade said impassively, "is that your elvan friends denied me passage through the Inner Zone."

"Well, yes," Shadow said hesitantly. "Laurel guessed who you were, or at least suspected."

"Indeed." Blade's voice dripped scorn. "I had wondered why I was not offered similar—hospitality."

"What, a bed companion?" Shadow asked, surprised. "That's nothing to do with *you*. My negligence, if anything. As your escort, if you wanted someone, you should have told me, and I'd have let them know. Elves stopped offering humans bed companions before the Black Wars. Humans seemed to get offended so easily by some of our customs! So we just stopped offering."

"Given elvan custom, I wonder the forest is not over-run," Blade said sarcastically.

"Well, it would be, if we littered incessantly like humans," Shadow said cheerfully. "But many of us are barren, and those who aren't come ripe only twice a century or so. If the Mother Forest hadn't given us a strong breeding drive, and if our customs didn't encourage it, we'd all have died out long ago."

"Are elves everywhere so?" Blade asked mockingly. "Or are our elves alone plagued with infertility?"

"Are they so what?" Shadow grinned. "No. Elves everywhere are different, just like humans. When Donya and I were traveling together we met dozens of other tribes of elves, and except for a few customs that seem to be common to everyone, like food and fire, they're no more like the elves in the Heartwood than you're like a cartwright in Mountaindale.

"Donya thinks that all elves came from the same place

long ago, and scattered out over the world like the humans have. That's why we all seem to have some things in common—language and a few customs, anyway. Different groups of elves faced different problems, of course, and lived in different ways, and that shaped them all. Our tribes, for example, isolated themselves and bred too closely before the Black Wars mixed us all together. Donya thinks that's why so many of us are barren, and why some of the tribes produced such short elves, like me.''

"Do you agree?''

Shadow shrugged. "I can't say that it really matters much. We are as we are, be it here or halfway across the world. I'll leave such problems to scholars. Elves aren't as interesting as humans. Humans are always changing things, always doing something new. Look at Allanmere. When I left, it was a little smattering of huts, a grazing common, and a half-built wall, and now look. All that in a few centuries! As for the elves in the Heartwood—well, if it hadn't been for the Black Wars, they'd still be doing the same things they did before, living the same way for the next thousand years.''

"You have little charity for your own people,'' Blade said.

"I love my people, what's left of them,'' Shadow said staunchly. "They're kind and strong and loyal to the core. But they're *boring,* and in over three centuries of travel I've seen things my kinfolk couldn't even dream of. I'm not the kind to dig my roots in deep. In time, Allanmere will get too small for me again and I'll move on to see what the rest of the world has been doing. It never stops, all the changing, and I want to see it.''

Shadow glanced sideways at her companion. "You've heard a great deal about me,'' she said. "Come on, assuage my insatiable curiosity and return the favor.''

Blade shrugged. "My life has been neither as interesting nor as pleasant as your own. Some you have guessed,'' she said. "Some rightly, some wrongly. The rest is better left unsaid. None of it matters, in the end, to any but myself.''

Shadow grimaced but did not press her.

''You haven't marked your road on here,'' she said, pulling out the map. ''Where will we come out?''

Blade pulled her ebony mount back and tapped a black-gloved finger on the map. ''Here,'' she said. ''Providing the road is as I remember it, and providing that flooding does not force us to detour.''

''That's not bad,'' Shadow said, pleased. ''From there it shouldn't be more than two days ride to Baloran's keep, if it's where I think it is. We should be able to make up the time we lost on our detour into the forest.''

''We will if your insatiable curiosity does not lead you to dance with any more fell-beasts,'' Blade mocked.

''I'll try to restrain myself,'' Shadow agreed good-naturedly. ''By Fortune's right hand, I've danced with handsomer partners, I'll admit.''

''Give me the map,'' Blade said, ''and I will draw the road.''

Shadow surrendered the rolled leather, and watched with interest as Blade roughed out a road with a charcoal-blackened stick, then drew an irregular oval near one loop of the road.

''This is Spirit Lake,'' Blade said, indicating the oval. ''The road will follow it for a time, so that we must camp nearby. Be warned, it is a dangerous place.''

''How could a lake that large be there, and nobody know about it?'' Shadow asked skeptically. ''It looks larger than Moon Lake in the Heartwood.''

''It is not large, except during the spring flooding,'' Blade said patiently. ''Then the rains and the flooding swell it, and things are disturbed from their rest in the hidden places of the swamp.''

''Isn't there any way around that area?'' Shadow asked.

''No. One must keep to the road,'' Blade said. ''There are pits of quicksand, sucking mud, and other dangers off the roads. We will have enough difficulty with your horses without tempting your goddess Fortune to smite us with her left hand.''

Shadow grimaced. Bad enough to have Blade for a traveling companion for so many days; worse yet to have to rely on her in a place Shadow knew nothing of, and one filled with dangers of which Blade might or might not choose to warn her.

To take her mind off such disheartening things, Shadow pulled out the bow and began carving.

''Are there shelters in the swamp?'' Shadow asked. ''I'd just as soon not sleep in the muck if we can help it.''

''There will be shelters, if they have stood,'' Blade mused. ''Not trail buildings as such, but shelters, yes. They will at least be some protection from the weather.''

''Mmm.'' Shadow sighed resignedly. It would have been pleasant to ride through the forest, to see the old familiar sights changed little in her absence, to smell the well-known smells and hear the birdsong. It would have been pleasant, too, to share food and fire with the odd patrol for the few days as they passed through, see the dances and trade news.

''Do you sing?'' Shadow asked abruptly.

''No,'' Blade said flatly. ''I do not. Why do you ask?''

''Well, you won't let *me* sing,'' Shadow said practically. ''It's just a way to pass the time.''

''I do not know,'' Blade said coldly, ''that the time needs passing.''

Shadow sighed again. It would be a long journey.

Blade's road—although Shadow hesitated to call it such—did not join the trail they had been riding on, but Blade led Shadow's mount by the reins through a twisting route until they finally came upon the almost-indiscernible, water-logged track.

The riding was much slower here, painstakingly winding around pools and mires, stopping periodically to let Shadow change horses while Blade sat impassively watching. By sundown Shadow was as exhausted as her animals.

"So where are these shelters?" she asked impatiently. "We can't ride in the dark, not here."

"The shelters will be farther along," Blade said. "We are still too near Allanmere. But there is a place not far ahead where we can camp."

They set up camp on a high hummock amid tumbled stone blocks. The ground was thoroughly damp from the rains, and there was no wood for a fire. Blackfell brought two fish and another eel, but Shadow declined to eat them raw, preferring her trail rations.

"You," Blade said pointedly, "are too choosy." She rinsed the fillet she had cut, sliced it into small strips, and nibbled at it indifferently.

"I'm not *that* hungry," Shadow chuckled. "You likened elves to the beasts in the forest, but we draw one difference—we bother to cook our catch."

"Given your cooking, I find it better raw," Blade said with a mirthless smile.

Shadow laughed.

"Donya used to tease me unmercifully about my cooking," she admitted. "I have to agree that if after five hundred years I haven't learned, I'm hopeless."

"That," Blade said, "is certain."

Shadow grinned, pleased that Blade had made something akin to a joke. The strange woman appeared in better humor now that they had left the forest and returned to the swamp, and Shadow hoped that her companion would prove more talkative and the journey less tedious than it had been so far.

"Your bow's coming well," she said. "I was lucky to find a good piece of wood so quickly. I've seen bowsmiths take days choosing a piece of wood."

Blade walked over to peer over Shadow's shoulder.

"You seem adept at carving," she said grudgingly.

"I used to think I'd become a wood carver," Shadow said proudly. "Back when I was still living in the Heartwood, our chief used to encourage me. It kept my hands busy, at least, and the rest of me still for a few hours," she added with a laugh. "Quite a feat, that."

"You were not training as a thief then?" Blade asked, glancing at her with that unnervingly probing expression. "I had thought it your life vocation."

Shadow shook her head, pleased at Blade's interest.

"How could they have trained me?" she asked. "There wasn't even an Allanmere then to speak of, let alone a Guild. My tribe would hardly have taught me to steal from them, and we didn't mix with the other tribes, so there was no such thing as a professional thief. Trespassing and poaching and spying, I'm afraid, is the best I could do then, but I did plenty of that."

"For your tribe?"

"For my own 'insatiable curiosity,'" Shadow corrected. "I guess even then I was leaning toward thievery, come to think of it. But it wasn't until a couple of centuries later that I took it up as a living."

Blade did not prompt her to continue, but her expression was not totally disinterested, and Shadow decided that the sound of her own voice was better than silence.

"When I left the Heartwood, I traveled east," she said. "Sneaking around the woods through everyone's tribal boundaries, I sometimes heard rumors of what the border tribes had seen. None of the humans who ventured into the Heartwood ever made it as far as the Western Heart—Songwater, now, that is—before some elvan patrol either killed them or chased them out of the woods. I was excited at the idea of seeing humans, maybe even walking among them, and I had a vague idea of selling my carvings to earn a living.

"By the time I reached my first human city the idea had lost a lot of its charm," Shadow continued wryly. "The first humans I met were highwaymen. They beat me senseless and took all my carvings, everything else I had. I couldn't even understand their language. I'd have gone back to the forest after that, but it was too far to make it without tools, weapons, or food. Fortunately a caravan of human pilgrims took me in and took me as far as Wyndermere, which was a good-sized city then. By the time we got there I'd picked up a little of the humans' language, not to mention a few hundred fleas from a couple of the pilgrims. Apparently the tenets of their religion didn't include bathing. They gave me a little money, though, and a lot more information, I think, than they intended.''

"Wyndermere," Blade mused. "That city was burned and sacked by the wave of barbarians moving south during the Black Wars, was it not?"

"The very same," Shadow nodded. "But at the time it wasn't too much different from Allanmere—smaller, fewer temples, fewer elves, and no real Guild, but otherwise not much different.

"Wyndermere was where I started stealing," Shadow sighed. "It was that or whoring, and I hadn't been that impressed with my first sample of humans as bedmates. I had no training, though, and I was miserable at it. Seemed like I was forever getting beaten around by somebody— better thieves, the people I was trying to rob, constables. I thought as soon as I got enough money to buy weapons and a little food, I'd head back to the Heartwood, but I couldn't even seem to manage to do that. Whoring started to look better every day.

"Then one day I met an old, old elf in the beggars' plaza," Shadow said. "His name was Doreth, and he'd once been a thief before age and a strange crippling disease had ruined his bones. He struck me a bargain—that he'd teach me the art if I'd turn over half my take to him every day. I agreed—why not?—and ended up staying in Wyndermere for more than forty years while Doreth taught me. Quite an education, too.

"Doreth died about three years before the Black Wars came to Wyndermere," Shadow said, shaking her head sadly in recollection. "The last five years we'd spent most of our money on healers for him, but it didn't do much good—he had almost twenty centuries, and enough is enough. Then his mind started to fail, and he decided too much was too much. I spent the last of my money on the best poison to be bought, and he thanked me for it. It was quick, at least, and painless.

"After that I didn't want to stay in Wyndermere, even though they'd started up a Guild by then, and I moved east. Good thing for me, too," Shadow remembered. "If I'd stayed, or gone north, I'd have been killed with the rest when the horde from the north came through. As it was, I was far out of their path by then, following rumors of the sea. Imagine, a body of water so vast that nobody knew what was on the other side! I traveled with caravans, mostly, stealing enough at the towns to pay my way or doing odd jobs to earn my keep. Then I traveled along the coast for a few years, enjoying the sea and learning my trade. When I learned about the wars I came back west, but seeing what had been left behind elsewhere—"

Shadow was silent for a long moment.

"Anyway, by that time I was a good enough thief," she said, changing the subject, "that I could support myself wherever I went, and that's what I did—traveled from town to town, Guild to Guild. That was quite an education, too. Do you know, you can walk into a human city, get to know it, go away, come back a hundred years later and it's a completely different place?"

"Mmm," Blade said noncommittally. She stared out at the night. "Had you blood kin in the Heartwood? Before the wars?"

"All the Silverleafs were blood kin, more or less," Shadow shrugged. "In the sense you mean, my mother Elia, her brother Frost, my mother's mother Cenda. I was a High Circle baby, so my father could have been any of a dozen men. Plenty of friends, a few lovers, and a fellow I might have possibly mated one day. None of them survived. Not surprising; the horde came through the western half of the forest, nearest the swamp, and very few elves from those areas survived. Western Heart was right in the path, and from what I hear, Silverleaf was one of the tribes that refused to join with the others. Stupid of them.''

''Sometimes it is easier to fight alone than to trust a stranger,'' Blade said remotely.

''Well, that may be, but it didn't work for the Silverleafs,'' Shadow shrugged. ''Personally I find it safer to let a lot of big, overmuscled, armored humans get hacked at instead of me.''

''Thus your association with Lady Donya.''

Shadow laughed. ''Don't let Donya hear you say that,'' she grinned. ''I don't think she'd find the description too flattering. She does have a tendency to think I need protecting, though—as the present case illustrates pretty well.''

Blade smiled coldly. ''What does she think she will do, storm his keep with her guard?''

''No, she'll read a proclamation first, and *then* storm the keep,'' Shadow sighed. ''That's why I want to get there first. I don't know whether it's because she's been cooped up in town playing Heir for so long, or because being Heir has gone to her head, but she's gone mist-headed if she thinks two squadrons of the guard are going to impress a mage like Baloran.''

''And how do *you* plan to get it?'' Blade asked mildly.

''That mainly depends on what you're doing,'' Shadow grinned. ''I'm sure you'll get in somehow. If you can get in, I can; and if you're there, I'm sure Baloran will be well distracted.''

''Ah, letting someone else do your work for you again,'' Blade said flatly. ''Well, it is no matter to me what you do. I am there to find Baloran, not your gem, and as you say, I will most likely be something of a—distraction—to him.''

''Bet on it,'' Shadow chuckled.

FIVE

"I don't like the look of this," Shadow said, and shivered.

There was little to like. Spirit Lake sprawled ahead of her and to the west like a rotting behemoth. The water was dead black in the sunless mist of the swamp; black as Blade's eyes and every bit as chilling. Steam coiled slowly up from the surface of the water. The few trees or bushes at the edge of the lake were twisted, gray and dead, or shimmering yellow-gray with corpse-light lichens. No reeds or swamp grass fringed the black shore; Shadow told herself that it was because the usual shore plants were drowned under the expanded boundaries of the flood-swollen lake, but a part of her believed the lake was simply deadly to anything living near its waters. No croakers sang evensong here; no birds dug for food in the black mud; no fish jumped; no silverwings skimmed the lusterless surface of the lake. A thick gray smell of mold and rot hung heavy in the fog.

"The vapors are unhealthy"—Blade shrugged—"and those who dwell here long sicken and die, but Spirit Lake has been here always. There is nothing living in it to fear. There is nothing living in it at all."

"How do you know that?" Shadow asked, grimacing at the water. "How can anybody stand to get close enough to it to find out? It stinks like last year's cesspits."

"When the shores advance, the plants and leaves rot under the water," Blade said absently. "When the floods come, deadly substances are washed up from the soil to foul the water, which usually comes up from hot springs under the ground. The water is too warm and too brackish to support life. Everything that drinks of it dies."

Blade's willingness to explain surprised Shadow.

"Why was it named Spirit Lake, then?"

Blade shrugged. "Because the mist rising from the lake resembles spirits, perhaps," she said. "Legends say that the lake is the dwelling place of evil spirits, who wait here to lure the unwary to their deaths."

"Do you believe that?" Shadow asked, glancing from the lake to her companion. She shivered again.

"I believe that lake has claimed many lives and will doubtless claim more," Blade said coldly. "Whatever its power, my belief or disbelief is no excuse for a lack of caution."

Shadow sighed, finding Blade's words little comfort. She unrolled the map.

"According to your map, there should be one of the shelters you mentioned soon," she said. "How long, do you think? My horses are tired, and I'm hungry."

"An hour, a little more," Blade said. "It is not far— there, see?"

Shadow squinted into the mists in the direction indicated by Blade's black-gloved finger. Were there some ill-defined, dark shapes around the curve of the lakeshore, or was it only her imagination?

"If you say so," Shadow said dubiously.

"Keep your horse on Blackfell's tracks," Blade said, urging her mount on even as she spoke. "There is sucking mud in these parts, and sometimes pockets of gas that causes faintness. If the lake water even enters a cut or sore, it will spread infection and disease. Above all, do not let your horse drink, no matter how it thirsts, or drink yourself."

"Bet on it," Shadow said uneasily, glancing at the still surface. She was not tempted. She nudged the roan sharply onto Blade's trail.

For once, Shadow was grateful for her chancy companion. The road, if indeed there was one, was apparently discernible only to Blade. The assassin led her a circuitous route, taking winding detours for no apparent reason—not apparent, at least, until Shadow would smell a faint odor of dizzying gas or see a half-rotted animal carcass in bubbling mud. A lukewarm drizzle began again, but she was already too soaked by the fog to bother with a cloak. Shadow soon ceased to look at the lake altogether, too concerned with following exactly upon the heels of Blade's mount. This was no place for a child of the Mother Forest to be, this foul place that was as deadly to the spirit as to the body.

Thus Shadow's roan nearly collided with the black rump of Blade's "horse" when it halted; the terrified roan instantly danced back and startled the bay, then slid precariously in the mud, nearly spilling Shadow from its back. Shadow clung grimly until the roan quieted, then glanced at what lay ahead.

Five middle-sized humps rose like giant warts from the surface of the swamp. Once their surface had been covered with grass, discernible now only as a slimy matting. Blade dismounted and stood waiting until Shadow did the same.

"Those aren't much shelter," Shadow said dubiously. "There isn't even enough flat space on top for a decent camp."

Blade smiled oddly and gestured Shadow around the side of one of the humps. Blade took a stick and poked around the lower surface of the hump until something moved, then pushed the door inward.

"Blackfell," she said, and the demon appeared at her side. Blade gestured at the door, and the demon bent without a word to step inside. It reappeared a moment later and held the door open mutely.

Shadow pulled a lantern from one of her saddlebags and,

despite the drizzle and fog, managed to light it as Blade waited impatiently. Abruptly Blade stepped through the low door, and Shadow followed, the light held out in front of her like a weapon against the dark interior.

To Shadow's surprise, the half-globe shelter was constructed not of curving wood ribs as she had expected, but of stone so exquisitely fitted that it seemed as though each piece had grown in its place for just that purpose. The door was, amazingly, also of stone, perfectly balanced to open smoothly. The grass obviously had grown from sods laid over the stone, not thatching. The interior of the shelter was as featureless as the outside, but the raised floor was also made of fitted blocks, and was perfectly dry. Perhaps most amazing of all were the carvings on the curved walls—not illustrations, but ornate patterns of lines and curves. Shadow ran her hand over them wonderingly, then whistled in awe. Had they indeed been carved? she wondered, for the stone was so perfectly smoothed that not one chisel stroke could be discerned, almost as if the designs had been melted in instead.

There were several small piles of wood—broken furniture, perhaps—scattered here and there, and a firepit at the center. Blade located the smokehole using Shadow's lantern, poking it clear with the stick, and Shadow hurried to lay a fire in the pit.

"Well, you can cook your food tonight," Blade mocked, "if Blackfell can find anything wholesome to eat in this area."

"It doesn't matter," Shadow said, sighing with relief as she raised her hands to the growing flames. "All I want is to be dry, really dry!"

"Best tend your horses first," Blade said dryly. "If they hunger and thirst, they may well go in search of that which will serve them ill." She sat down by the fire, moving close to the flames and almost smiling herself.

Shadow sighed resignedly and pushed the door open,

relieved that at least the tired roan and bay had stood still and not wandered off into the mist.

Shadow poured grain onto a sack laid flat on the ground, knowing the horses would need more than a nosebag and unwilling to let the grain touch the foul mud. The water was a little more complicated, but at last the horses had their fill from the cooking pot while Shadow rubbed them down. She started to unfasten the saddlebags.

"Shadow," a voice whispered.

Shadow whirled around, dreading to see Blade's demon when she was alone, but there was no one there—or was that a vague figure a few feet off in the mist?

"Who is it?" Shadow said, her voice unsteady.

"Child," the voice said chidingly. "Don't you know me?"

Shadow trembled violently. "Mother?" She whispered. "Mother?"

The figure came closer, became clearer. Small Elia had been, almost as small as Shadow, but frail, reed-slender, ethereal as mist, her hair ghost-pale, her eyes the delicate blue of a summer sky, her slow movements as graceful and flowing as a dance. Her smile was as serene and beautiful as ever.

"Mother?" Shadow whispered again. "But—"

"We came here to hide from the wars," Elia murmured, her voice as familiar a music as the chuckle of a forest stream. Her hands closed warm on Shadow's. "Only a few of us. We came here to be safe, here where no one would come. It was our only refuge. We've been waiting here for you such a long, lonely time."

Dim figures appeared behind her, slowly, from the mist.

"Cenda and Frost are here with me," Elia said softly. "And your friends, Bramble and Rietta and Noriss and Heather, all waiting for you."

"When I heard about the wars I thought I'd never come back," Shadow murmured, unaware of the tears flowing down her cheeks. "I didn't want to know you were all dead—know for sure. I wanted to believe you were all alive, all safe, always there in the forest waiting.''

''We would never leave you behind,'' Elia said fondly. ''My only, beloved daughter, we could never have gone to the Mother Forest and left you alone.''

And there they all were—Wiryn, her first lover; Rowena, who had taught her to use the bow and knife; Ivy, Shadow's childhood companion in mischief; Solan, who had once asked Shadow to be his mate and had understood when she said no—and now she could hear the music and the laughter, the distant voices of her tribe raised in song, smell the sweet aromas of a feast cooking over the firepits.

Shadow shook her head to clear it, her brow wrinkling. Why was it strange that they were here, that the fires were burning—if she could just remember—

''But don't you see, you've come home,'' Elia said soothingly, wrapping a warm, slender arm around Shadow's waist. ''Come and join the celebration, and sing us the story of your adventures. There is wine waiting, and food. We have been waiting so long for you, so long, and now you've come home, Shadow, at last—''

Shadow reached for their hands hesitantly. Something—something important—

''Come, Shadow,'' Frost said kindly, his white hair sparkling in the moonlight. ''We're all waiting for you.''

But—

''No,'' Shadow whispered, shaking her head violently. ''No, I'm not—''

''Come, child,'' Elia murmured. ''Come and be with us, come home.''

Truth seared through her in an agonizing fire.

''My name's not Shadow!'' she screamed, sobbing at her loss. ''You never called me that!''

Silence.

Shadow knuckled the tears from her eyes, gasping, choking down her sobs.

There was no one there.

"Shadow?" a voice called. Clear this time, and close. "Shadow, help! Hurry! I need help!"

"Doe?" Shadow called, confused. "Where are you?"

"Over here!" Donya called. "I can hear your voice, but I can't see you! Hurry, I'm sinking!"

Shadow could dimly see a shape ahead, low to the ground, thrashing. She hurried forward, snatching her belt free.

"Doe?" she called. "Don't struggle, you'll sink faster! Try to lie flat if you can!"

"I can't!" Donya shouted back. "My armor's too heavy! Hurry!"

Shadow sprinted forward, only to pull up sharply, nearly choking as an iron grip seized her collar and pulled her backward.

"You little fool!" Blade hissed in her face. "Have you lost your wits?"

"Shadow!" Donya screamed, despair now in her voice.

"Let me go," Shadow said desperately. "She's sinking— get a rope—"

"Idiot!" Blade snapped. "There is no one there; look for yourself!"

Shadow gaped blankly. She was standing at the very edge of Spirit Lake, the slimy water lapping at her boots. Nothing but mist could be seen rising from the surface of the water.

"But I—I heard Donya," Shadow mumbled confusedly.

"You heard nothing, for there is nothing there," Blade said exasperatedly. "I heard *you,* talking and shouting and weeping, and here you are, acting like a cloud-headed dolt and doing precisely what I told you *not* to do. Now come into the shelter and stay there, for I will not rescue you from your own foolishness again."

Trembling violently, Shadow followed Blade quickly to the shelter, picking up the saddlebags as she went. As an afterthought, she tied the horses' leads firmly to a rock before she hurried into the shelter.

Blade seated herself by the door, giving Shadow a

pointed glare. Shadow paid no heed, hurriedly stripping off
her wet clothes and laying them to dry by the fire. Even
sitting near the flames, wrapped in her blanket, she could
not stop trembling.

"You are indeed Fortune's favored one if you have not
managed to take lung-rot or some other such ailment,"
Blade grumbled. She filled Shadow's mug from a skin of
wine left near the fire to heat and watched sternly as
Shadow drank it all. "Warm yourself and eat, for I have no
desire to tend you should you fall ill."

Shadow glanced at the two eels roasting over the fire and
shuddered, reaching instead for the wineskin. Only the heat
of the mulled wine kept her from pouring it down her throat,
but she had swallowed nearly half the skin before Blade
snatched it disgustedly away.

"Oh, Fortune favor me, let be," Shadow grumbled. "I
won't get drunk on half a skin of mulled wine. I'm just cold
and shaken, that's all. Tell me some of those legends you
mentioned, about the lake."

Blade poured herself a mug of the hot wine and skewered
a piece of eel on her knife.

"Long before there were humans here," she said, "perhaps before there were even elves here, there were others.
No one knows who they were, but it is believed they came
from the west, because while others have found some of
their traces to the west, none have ever been found farther
east than this."

"What traces?" Shadow asked.

Blade gestured absently at their shelter.

"This is one," she said. "Whoever they were, they were
unparalleled stonemasons. These shelters have lasted centuries upon centuries, and still they stand untouched. Travelers use them and—others at times. It is believed they were
built by magic, perhaps. No drop of water leaks in, no
whisper of wind or snow. You can see how perfectly the
stones are fitted—almost as if they grew together."

"That's just what I thought," Shadow mused, calming

somewhat in her curiosity. "Those carvings, too—they seem too smooth."

Blade shrugged.

"Whoever they were, they came from dry country, that can be seen," she said. "No one knowledgeable about this land would have built so near to the lake and the river, for it was certain these lands would flood, and while the shelters themselves would stay dry, the surrounding lands would not. They could not raise a crop, and there was nothing else but fish to be had. Still they lived here some time, for they built many other things in the swamp here and there.

"Here they died, it is believed, for there is no evidence they went elsewhere. Possibly it was a disease, such as drylanders seem to get when they come to a wet place, or possibly a disaster, such as the great fire which came to the Heartwood two decades ago. Or perhaps it was another wave of barbarians such as those who came in the Black Wars who killed them. I am inclined to think the latter, for there have been traces found of such a battle—fragments of weapons and such things.

"At any rate they died, these strangers, leaving their traces on the land. If they died in a war, perhaps it was their magic, or that of the barbarians, which cursed Spirit Lake. Perhaps they created the spirits of the lake to use as a weapon against the invaders, or perhaps they were all slaughtered and this is their spirits' vengeance. No one knows, but that is the legend."

"But I didn't see strangers," Shadow protested. Hesitatingly, she told Blade what she'd seen.

"Surely you cannot believe you saw the spirits of your kin, and especially the Lady Donya, who is not even dead, most likely," Blade said contemptuously. "Obviously you saw images created from your own mind, images that the lake spirits believed would draw you to them. Your kin, because you had recently spoken of them and therefore thought of them; Lady Donya, because she is your dear friend and one you would be most likely to throw aside caution to rescue.''

''But what do the spirits get out of my dying?'' Shadow asked. ''I mean, alive or dead, what use am I to them?''

''You ask me?'' Blade sneered. ''I could tell you something of demons, perhaps, and much of death, but nothing of whatever dwells in that lake. I have the most important knowledge, and that is that it is well to avoid the place in general, and the lake in particular.''

''That's odd,'' Shadow mused. ''I thought I'd heard every legend the elves told about the swamp—and I know the elves avoided the Reaches like a plague pit, but they didn't know much, either. How did you hear that story?''

Blade shrugged. ''The elves, perhaps, do not know everything,'' she said indifferently.

''Apparently not,'' Shadow said. She reached for a piece of eel. ''But I'd *still* like to know where you heard that story.''

''Go to sleep,'' Blade said abruptly, turning away. ''We will start early.''

''Whatever you say,'' Shadow shrugged, glad enough to curl up in the warmth of her bedroll. Blade's mood had apparently changed, and in a way she didn't much like. The combination of the wine, however, and the aftermath of her nerve-racking experience precluded much worrying. She was asleep almost immediately.

Something was wrong. Shadow sat up in the darkness of the shelter, wondering what had wakened her. There was only the dimmest of light from the low fire, but Shadow could see that Blade was not in her pallet, which, to all appearances, had not been slept in.

Shadow sat silently, listening intently. She could hear her horses, snorting unhappily in the damp night. Other than that there was the uncanny silence of Spirit Lake—no peepers, no croakers, no crickets, nothing—

—then a howl, a horrible, despairing howl that could have come from no human throat.

Blade was out there, somewhere, with that howl.

Shadow crawled out of her pallet, hesitated only a moment, then drew her knife and hurried outside.

Mist and more mist. She could hardly see her horses, let alone Blade. The horses' snorts seemed to echo off the fog.

A small sound now, perhaps a sob.

''Fortune favor me,'' Shadow muttered uneasily. Blade or another trap? And if Blade, did she want to be found? What might she do if she did not?

Again, Shadow hesitated only a moment before she plunged into the mist.

In an instant she was lost, or would have been had it not been for the clearly audible whuffling of the horses. There were no other sounds in the misty dark except for the faint sound of dripping water.

Then there was another faint sound, even less than before—perhaps only the rustle of clothing or a hiss of breath—but it was enough for Shadow's sensitive ears. She imagined a line through the fog and, without another thought, followed it directly toward Spirit Lake.

Blade was there, on the shore, almost in the dank water. She was kneeling, facing away from Shadow, no more than a flash of pale skin in the darkness, her arms extended in front of her. Again there was the faintest sob.

Uneasily Shadow moved forward. Did she see shapes swirling in the mists? Resolutely she kept her eyes fastened on Blade's back as she stepped around to the side, her boots sinking deep in the foul-smelling mud.

Blade was staring fixedly into the stinking deadness of Spirit Lake, her eyes wide and dry. Her gloved hands were clasped tightly around the hilt of the black dagger, her arms knotted hard with tension. The point of the dagger was turned inward, almost touching Blade's abdomen. Her arms, her hands, the dagger, were all trembling violently. Again Blade made that strange sobbing sound, although no tears came.

If Shadow stopped to think, she might have reasoned that

in a struggle that black dagger might plunge into Blade's flesh before Shadow could stop her—or, in the process, Shadow herself. She might have reasoned that the two of them, grappling together, might fall into Spirit Lake.

Therefore, she did not stop to think; she simply reversed her knife and brought the hilt down on the back of Blade's head as sharply as she could, grasping the black leather of Blade's tunic and pulling her backward at the same time.

Blade made a surprised grunting sound and fell obligingly backward, the dagger still clenched in one black-gloved hand. Shadow hurriedly pried the deadly thing loose from her grasp and jammed it into its sheath, then dragged Blade backward through the mud, wheezing with effort, until she was a few yards from the lake. She let her limp burden fall to the mud and sat down beside Blade, panting hard.

"I know, I'll get a horse," Shadow muttered presently. "Then I can tie Blade with a rope and drag—no, if I go back to the horse I won't have any way of finding Blade, and no way to find my way back to the shelter. Forget that.

"All right. I'll tie a rope to Blade and go back and—no, rope's in the shelter. Forget that.

"All right, I'll just sit here all damned night and catch swamp rot," Shadow swore impatiently, "or until Blade wakes up and decides to slit my throat for idiotically preventing her from sticking a soul-sucking demon into her guts.

"All right, I'll—"

Shadow gingerly pulled the black dagger out of its sheath, dropping it immediately to the mud.

"Uh—you, Blackfell. I need some help here."

The dagger lay where it was, in the mud.

"Damn all, I can't carry her! She's half again as big as me! Come out of there and pick her up or she'll get lung-rot lying out here!"

Nothing.

"If you don't get out here, I'll throw you in the lake!"

Nothing.

"When Blade wakes up, I'll tell her whose fault it is she lay here in the mud all this time."

The dagger vanished, and the demon crouched in the mud, surveying Shadow through slitted eyes.

"Pick her up," Shadow said patiently, swallowing her fear. "And take her back to the shelter."

The demon silently lifted Blade as if she weighed nothing at all. Blade groaned faintly.

"Tough head," Shadow muttered. She listened for the roan's snort, then hurried back to the shelter with undue haste.

The demon dropped Blade to her pallet rather carelessly, then vanished. Shadow sighed, wet a cloth from her wineskin, and gently cleaned the swelling lump on the back of Blade's head. She picked up the dagger and moved it carefully out of reach, then sat down to wait.

There was no warning; Blade's eyes simply opened, clear and knowing, and her hand went to the dagger's sheath instantly.

"Wait," Shadow said hurriedly. "It's right over there." She pointed.

Blade glanced at the dagger, then at Shadow, saying nothing. She sat up, winced, and reached to gingerly touch the lump on her head. She frowned darkly.

"Sorry," Shadow said, grinning apologetically. "I think you were about to make a serious mistake."

"Blackfell," Blade said, her eyes locked on Shadow's. The dagger leaped into her hand. Blade held it for a long moment while Shadow held her breath; then she placed it silently back in its sheath. To Shadow's amazement, she spoke.

"You have," she said emotionlessly, "my thanks."

Shadow started to shrug it off with a joke; then she hesitated.

"Blade—what did you see that was so terrible?" she asked, greatly daring.

Blade turned her black eyes to Shadow, and Shadow was surprised at the ancient pain there.

"Myself," she said simply. Then she rolled over in her pallet, turning her back on Shadow without another word.

"What is it?" Donya asked, joining Captain Oram at the camp border. "The men are jumping at the slightest noise and I feel a little jumpy myself. I thought this night before reaching Baloran was supposed to make us more rested, but stopping this close to his place might be a mistake after all."

"It might," Captain Oram agreed. "There's—I don't know, something chancy in the air. The night sounds aren't right, not quite. I feel as though there's something hanging over us."

"Yes, exactly," Donya frowned. Oram had put name to the feeling that had plagued her all evening. "Do you think—"

"Double the watches," Oram nodded. "I don't think the men will mind at all, seems to me."

"I could—" Donya began, but Oram's face silenced her.

"No, you must rest, my lady," he said gently. "Tomorrow you must be fresh and confident and clear in thought."

Donya sighed and went to bed.

She awoke abruptly as a shriek ripped through the night like a knife through cloth.

Despite fifty guardsmen outside her tent, Donya still slept in her armor, and her sword was never far from her hand. Before the second shriek came, she was out of her tent and into the thick of battle. Her sword was swinging before she had a clear view of what she battled.

Had she delayed a moment, she might well have lost her courage, for the first fire-silhouetted view of her opponent caused her sword to falter momentarily.

Was it man or beast? Donya could not be sure. The creature walked on two legs like a man, but was bent and stooped rather than upright, its elongated upper limbs nearly brushing the ground. Fur half covered it in patchy mats, and its stubby fingers, flashing with amazing speed in battle, sported long and deadly claws. Its wolflike head had a shortness that made it look more human, but the muzzle contained a wolf's sharp and lethal teeth.

Its teeth were stained with human blood.

Her warrior's discipline did not fail her. In the heat of battle, fear and pain took their accustomed places at the back of her mind; her sword moved as a limb of her body, quicker than her thought. There could be no hesitation; she was a sword, bright and sharp, which only just happened to have at one end of it a fleshy form.

The creature howled again and leaped; Donya dropped to one knee, twisting rapidly as she did so, and the sword flashed in the firelight. The howl was cut off midway, and the wolf-thing fell past her, blood spraying from its nearly severed throat.

No time to think, no time to fear.

Donya swallowed, stood, and hastened toward the battle.

SIX

"You can't possibly be serious," Shadow said, staring.

The vast expanse of the Brightwater, brown-gray with mud and swollen with spring floods, lay before them.

"You can*not* be serious," Shadow repeated.

"Not here," Blade said impatiently. "The road follows the river north. There is a better place there. I would think you would be glad to leave the swamp."

"I am," Shadow said with feeling. Just the sight of blue sky, the smell of fresh air, and the sound of living things cheered her, although they would not actually be out of the Reaches for some hours.

They had left the shelter at the first hint of light two days ago, Blade seeming as anxious as Shadow to be quit of the place. Since then they had ridden as quickly as the weather and the trail would allow.

After her experience with Spirit Lake, Shadow soon came to a grudging appreciation of the swamp. It teemed with life, boiled over with living things in a way that even the forest never did. There were creatures living there the like of which Shadow had never seen before.

There were also more of the strange shelters along the road at irregular intervals—sometimes in groups, sometimes alone. The shelters became more frequent as the women left the area of Spirit Lake, and were welcome dry spots in the overfull marshes.

Blade knew at least as many things that could be picked, peeled, or dug up in the swamp as Shadow did in the forest, and every evening when they camped there would be fresh game of some sort or another—fish, eels, the odd marshco- ney, swamp birds, or, to Shadow's utter disgust, snakes. At least, to her great relief, the demon brought home no giant spiders or the like.

Also amazing to Shadow was that the Dim Reaches, for all their ill reputation, could be beautiful. As no further rains soaked the land and the Brightwater slowly receded, the late-spring sun was having its way with the plants of the swamp. A profusion of unusual flowers bloomed, colorful mushrooms—some tasty—popped up everywhere, and mul- ticolored lacewings flittered over the green surface of the water.

Still, there was little regret in Shadow's heart when she saw the shining expanse of the Brightwater ahead of her and contemplated leaving the swampland behind at last.

"So, I give up, where are we?" Shadow asked, pulling out the map. "I know we're way west of the forest, but how far?"

"We are here," Blade said, tapping a spot on the map. "Another day to reach the crossing. Half a day to cross, given the flooding. Three to cross the plains."

Shadow grinned hugely.

"You were right! We should have five days on Donya and her guard now, and that's without them being delayed anywhere or following a false trail, which they've got to do, whichever of those spots they pick first."

Then her grin faded.

"But how did we end up on the wrong side of the Brightwater? I mean, that swamp was pretty wet, but it wasn't the Brightwater."

"Nor is this," Blade said. "This is merely one of the

Brightwater's tributaries. It flows *under* the swamp, you see, then comes out again."

"It's not on the map," Shadow frowned.

"Neither was Spirit Lake," Blade shrugged. "No one comes through here, and no one needs to cross this tributary, so it is not mapped. Any fool could reason as much."

"Sorry, I'm just a city girl," Shadow shot back. "I don't tend to need maps. I don't tend to *use* maps. Or cross rivers, when I can help it."

"Then how have you done so much traveling?" Blade asked.

"Mostly in other people's caravans," Shadow sighed. "Preferably in the wagon of some well-favored, wealthy fellow with plenty of money and lots of wine."

"Well, this time you have only Blackfell and me for company," Blade said flatly, "and a river to cross. Therefore, we will make a boat and cross it."

"*Make* a *boat?*" Shadow demanded. She had a sinking feeling that what Blade had in mind was not a comfortable passenger barge or even a cargo ship. "Just like that? Make a boat? Can't your friend change into a dragon and fly us over or something?"

Blade scowled.

"If he could change into a dragon," she said impatiently, "we could have flown to Baloran's keep in a day. He has a few shapes which he has learned, and they are not far larger or far smaller than his own."

"Why's that?"

"As I said, I am no mage," Blade snapped. "And were I one, I would have better things to do than to answer your never-ending questions, which serve no purpose but to lengthen our journey."

"Then let's shorten it by riding while I ask my questions," Shadow grinned, urging the roan ahead. "The sooner we're across that river or tributary or whatever it is, the happier I'll be."

They reached the bank of the river by noon. An hour

before, Blade, to Shadow's surprise, dismounted and asked to ride the bay. Shadow agreed, to the bay's obvious displeasure, and Blade's black steed vanished. Shadow saw the black shape winging rapidly northward.

By this time Shadow knew better than to bother asking, but she was answered anyway. When they reached the edge of the river, the demon was waiting for them, and fifteen stout logs, bound with vines into a raft, lay ready on the bank. A forked log had been mounted at the back, and a large, roughly carven oar had been bound there as a sort of rudder.

"Don't we need something to paddle across with?" Shadow asked dubiously. "That oar on the back won't get us far."

"That is only for steering," Blade shrugged. "Blackfell?"

The demon vanished. In its place was a huge daggertooth, a gigantic scaled lizardlike creature the like of which Shadow had seen only in the warm southern regions. But no daggertooth Shadow had ever seen gleamed black from the tip of its razor-toothed snout to the end of its plated tail, nor had she ever seen one so large. It weighed, she surmised, almost as much as the horse.

Blade took the coil of rope from her saddlebags and, without asking, Shadow's rope as well. She fastened both ropes securely to the two corners of the raft closest to the water. The daggertooth crawled between the ropes, and Blade set about tying the leads into a sort of sturdy harness that ran before, behind, and between the daggertooth's front legs.

Despite the early hour, Blade deemed it too late to attempt a crossing then; Shadow, who was thoroughly sick of the swamp, would have preferred to risk it despite her hatred of boats and rivers, but deferred to Blade's greater knowledge.

Camping by the river carried the bonuses of fresh—if muddy—water and plentiful fish. While Blackfell made their evening catch, Shadow set a few lines and caught several more fish and three eels.

"The pleasures of an underfished section of river," Shadow said cheerfully, cleaning her catch as well as the two large fish and the webfoot Blackfell brought back.

"If you eat all of that," Blade noted sarcastically, "we will need a larger raft to bear your weight tomorrow, and your girth will be greater than your paltry height."

"I'm going to half smoke the fish," Shadow said sagely. "Then I can pack them in salt and they'll stay fresh for a long time. They'll be better than trail rations if we can't hunt, and they'll be good straight from the pouch, too."

"Do that," Blade agreed, reaching for the webfoot. "And Blackfell will prepare the fowl, so that I know that at least tonight I am assured of *edible* food."

"It's bad," Captain Oram said quietly.

Donya slumped where she stood, letting Ambaleis support her weight against his sweating shoulder. Blood drenched her, some of it her own; her armor was soiled and dented.

"How bad?" she asked wearily.

"We lost fifteen men," Oram said. "Two more may not survive. A dozen are wounded, some badly."

Donya sighed, resting her face in her bloody hands. "How many can go on?" she asked.

"Twenty-five," Oram said. "That's not the problem."

Donya looked up, brushing the limp hair out of her eyes. "What's the problem?"

"Horses," Oram said quietly. "Those things weren't even after us; they were after our horses. There's only ten. Plus yours, of course."

"Gods!" Donya pounded her fist against Ambaleis's sturdy side. "By the time we get there walking it'll be sunset."

She was silent for a long moment. "No," she said at last. "We go on. The others will catch up when they can."

"My lady!" Oram protested, shocked. "You cannot think to march on Baloran with only ten men!"

"We can't wait," Donya told him. "If we get closer and stop again, we'll meet more of those beasts, or worse. I've got to meet with Baloran tomorrow, and get out of his lands as quickly as possible. There's no time to wait, and there's no other choice."

There was a little rain that night, which was not entirely unexpected, but it worried Shadow and even Blade seemed concerned; Shadow prayed that the river would not be so swollen in the morning that they dared not cross, or, worse, might have to backtrack and find another way. Blade got up in the middle of the night to pull the raft up farther on the shore, with the demon to help her.

The river was, indeed, higher in the morning, but not too much so, and Blade decided they would attempt the crossing.

"Help me to push the raft farther out," Blade said. "It must be ready to launch before we put your horses on it, or Blackfell cannot pull it into the water."

Shadow grimaced but lent her small strength to forcing the raft into the water. When it bobbed uneasily in the strong current, only one edge resting lightly on the sandy bottom, Blade stopped, not releasing her hold on the raft, and gestured with her head at Shadow's horses.

The bay, though obviously frightened, was docile enough; the unhappy roan, however, had other ideas. She danced backward, showing the whites of her eyes and squealing, when Shadow tried to lead her onto the makeshift craft.

"Hurry," Blade growled. "This raft will begin to drift soon. If you cannot control the beast, I will have Blackfell subdue it."

"Relax," Shadow shrugged. "Demons and rivers aren't my areas of knowledge, but I do know animals, at least."

Shadow led the roan away from the river, talking to it soothingly, breathing into its nostrils (she had to stand on

tiptoe) until it calmed. She pulled out a bit of dried fruit and
fed it to the horse, then pulled out a cloth and blindfolded
the beast while it chewed. She led the now-quiet horse back
to the raft, where it allowed itself to be led onto the platform
and placed next to the bay with no further trouble.

"Hobble it," Blade suggested, letting go of the raft and
climbing aboard.

Shadow shook her head.

"That river looks bad," she said. "If something happens
to the raft, after all this rain, she'll need to be able to swim."

Blade grunted and moved to the back of the raft. The
black daggertooth was swimming strongly across the current, its tail lashing furiously. Nonetheless, they were
drifting slightly downstream. Blade moved to the mounted
oar, angling it into the water and digging in, and the raft's
course corrected slightly.

Shadow glanced uneasily at the far bank. It seemed
terribly distant.

"There aren't any rocks in this river, are there?" she
asked nervously. "I mean, rocks that the raft might hit and
bust apart?"

Blade shook her head.

"No rocks. The bottom here is mostly mud and silt,
stirred up by the flood. Of course—"

The raft suddenly jarred, nearly throwing Shadow over
the side, bumped over something, then settled back into its
smooth movement.

"—there are submerged stumps, this time of year, and
floating logs."

"Oh, really?" Shadow said sarcastically, trying desperately to clutch at both the raft and the horses' lead ropes.
She watched the daggertooth cut swiftly through the muddy
water.

"What did we need the raft for anyway?" she asked.
"That thing could have carried both of us over on its back,
and flown back for the saddlebags, too."

"And we could have carried your horses over in our

pockets, perhaps?'' Blade mocked. ''Or perhaps you, with
your remarkable gift with animals, could simply have stood
on the far bank and whistled, and they would jump in and
swim over prettily.''

''All right, all right,'' Shadow grumbled. ''But I *hate*
boats. And rafts. And Fortune-be-damned flooded rivers.''

''Ah, what happened to the contented elf? Fine day,
sweet-smelling air, fine horse, and all that?''

''I'd trade the lot for solid, dry ground under my feet,''
Shadow mumbled. ''A cheery inn, a good fire, a hot meal,
a soft bed—''

''And a man between your legs, no doubt,'' Blade
snapped. ''That energy would be better used if you would
lend your strength to help me steer, unless you want us
carried leagues out of our way.''

Shadow reluctantly joined Blade at the back of the raft,
leaning against the oar as she saw Blade doing.

''How do you know which way to steer this raft?'' she
asked.

''Blackfell sees the obstacles,'' Blade panted. ''Then
I—left!''

Shadow hurriedly corrected as Blade did, breaking into a
cold sweat as the powerful current twisted the oar violently,
nearly knocking Shadow into the swirling water.

''Then I know,'' Blade finished. ''Straighten it out now.''

Shadow obeyed grimly, her arms trembling with the
strain. Their strength seemed insignificant against the might
of the river. As they entered the main stream of the river,
there were more logs. They bumped against the raft, causing
it to shiver and jolt. Several times Shadow nearly lost her
balance between the drag of the current, the jolting of the
raft, and the increasingly wet and slippery footing.

''I can't keep this up much longer,'' Shadow panted.

''You need not.'' Blade sounded nearly as winded as she.
''There is an island slightly downstream. We will stop there
to rest and eat before we continue.''

Shadow glanced over her shoulder. Indeed there was a

small island not far away, and the daggertooth was pulling
the raft toward it, allowing the current's downstream push to
help them now.

The sight of land, any land, cheered Shadow, and she bent
to the rudder with renewed energy. Even so, it seemed like
an eternity before she felt the raft grate against the river
bottom. The island, Shadow suspected, was partly submerged due to the flooding; bushes and low scrub were
growing right down to the waterline, some drowning in the
muddy water of the river.

"Get out and get your horses off," Blade snapped.
"Blackfell will pull the raft to the other side, and we must
be there to pull it in and tie it up."

Shadow nodded and released the rudder oar gratefully.
The stupid bay was placid as usual and the roan did not
struggle, but seemed almost as glad as Shadow to be off the
raft; it stood shaking and exhausted as Shadow removed its
blindfold.

"I'm about worn out," Shadow panted.

"We cannot rest yet." Blade turned and pushed into the
scrub; Shadow sighed unhappily and followed, pulling the
horses after her.

The river was apparently not as high as it had been;
Shadow found herself maneuvering through mud-stained
bushes that occasioned equally mud-stained clothing, slipping through deposits of river silt and thin mud. She took
some satisfaction, however, in noting that Blade's dignified
black leather tunic and trousers were as stained and be-
grimed as her own.

"Slow down!" Shadow wheezed as Blade pushed ahead,
nearly out of sight.

"Catch up when you can," Blade snapped back impatiently. "You can hardly get lost on this small island."

Shadow heard her crashing recklessly through the bushes
ahead, and she stopped, waving a resigned hand after her.

"Never mind," Shadow gasped, sitting down on a fallen

log. "Not another step. Not another Fortune-be-damned *step* until I've had some wine!"

Shadow had no more than pulled out her wineskin, however, when a cry of mingled anger and pain came from ahead of her. Shadow wearily stood back up and pushed forward.

"Probably fell into a mud pit," she said resignedly, "or slid down an embankment right into the river, and if she thinks I'm going to dive in after—"

"Hurry, damn you!"

Blade's voice came from quite nearby; so near, in fact, that Shadow nearly tripped over her when she parted the bushes and stepped into a muddy clearing strewn with flood-deposited branches and litter. Blade was sprawled on the ground, cutting clumsily at the leather at the back of her right thigh with a plain knife.

"What's the matter?" Shadow asked perplexedly. "Did you sprain something?"

"Mist-headed idiot!" Blade snapped. "I've been stung by a digger worm. Now cut the damnable thing out before it digs in too deep!"

Digger worm! Shadow swallowed hard even as she bent to help, taking the knife from Blade and slicing through the tough leather. Digger worms were one of the dangers of the Dim Reaches, much feared though seldom found. These parasites reproduced by pushing into animal flesh—living or dead—with their tough, sharp heads and burrowing deep, then depositing its eggs at some point and continuing on. If it was not cut out before the eggs were deposited, the affected limb was usually amputated as a precaution; for once the eggs hatched, as they would in but a day or two, the larvae would begin likewise burrowing through the victim's flesh, eating until they grew to a sufficient size to chew their way free, mate, dig a hole in the mud, wait for a new victim, and begin the cycle anew. If the burrowing of the initial parent did not kill the host, the larvae almost invariably did.

Shadow finished cutting the leather away, then dropped

Blade's muddy knife on the ground and drew her own, which was both cleaner and sharper. She pulled out her wine flask, sighing at the sacrifice, and liberally splashed the wine over the blade.

She hesitated, surprised at the sight of Blade's skin. Blade's face had been pale enough—come to think of it, Shadow'd not seen so much of an inch of her elsewhere—but the skin at the back of her thigh was almost *gray*, uncannily smooth but tough to the touch.

"Well, what are you waiting for?" Blade growled. "Your knife is not pleasant to anticipate. I would prefer that you hurry before my leg is forfeit."

"Uh—yes, of course." Shadow bit her lip and sliced into Blade's thigh over the small puncture. Blade's blood oozed oddly dark and sluggish.

At the first cut, Blade swore once and all her muscles tightened, but she did not move.

"Have you got it?" she asked from between clenched teeth.

"Not yet." Shadow winced sympathetically as she dug deeper with her knife. "Sorry."

"Save your pity and hurry," Blade gritted out. "Well that your knife is so sharp, but its caress is not so sweet I would prolong it."

Shadow nodded and cut ruthlessly, wondering a little at Blade's stoic tolerance of the treatment. Blood was flowing freely now, and a thought flashed through Shadow's mind that there was a great deal of difference between plunging a knife into an enemy in the heat of a fight and cold-bloodedly slicing into one's traveling companion.

"There it is!" Shadow crowed. Tugging the slippery creature, with its backward-barbed spines, free of Blade's flesh doubtlessly hurt worse than the quick cutting, but other than one gasped oath in some language Shadow did not recognize, Blade made no reaction.

"Well, kill the damned thing," Blade croaked, "and make sure it's not left eggs in my leg."

"Right."

Shadow hurriedly crushed the worm with the end of a stick, then reached for her waterskin and a skin of brandy.

"Hold on," she told Blade. "I've got to wash the blood away so I can see."

"I hardly wish to hear the agenda," Blade said sarcastically, pain lending an edge to her voice. "Do it and be done."

Shadow washed the wound first with water and then the brandy; at the touch of the alcohol Blade shuddered, but Shadow relievedly reported the wound clean.

"I'll have to sew it, though," she said unhappily. "I *hate* sewing wounds. Had to learn how, though, traveling with Donya."

"Well, neither of us need suffer your sewing *this* one," Blade growled. "Hold it closed and be quiet for a moment. Blackfell—"

The demon appeared with alarming suddenness by Shadow's side, almost startling her into releasing her pressure on the deep cut. The demon laid its hands on either side of Shadow's for a moment, and Shadow felt the flesh under her hand grow momentarily hot; Blade screamed once, hoarsely. Then the demon vanished and Blade was pulling impatiently away from her.

Shadow stared blankly. Blade's skin was covered with blood, but it was whole, with only a red scar.

"You didn't tell me you were a healer," she said wonderingly. "Fortune favor me, you put Auderic to shame!"

"I am no healer," Blade snarled. "It is no different than if the wound healed with time, but that I used the time of others instead of my own. I dislike to do it, for it costs me dear in that which is difficult for me to gain. Now give me peace from your endless questions and let us get to the other side of the island before our raft, which Blackfell had to abandon, floats away and leaves us to swim the river!"

Blade scrambled to her feet, grimacing with pain, and

limped away; Shadow gaped after her a moment, then picked up Blade's dagger and her own, reclaimed the horses, and hurried after her.

The raft had not drifted away, to Shadow's relief; indeed, it was partly drawn up on the ground and the harness tangled in a bush.

"Now, can we *please* have a moment to rest and eat?" Shadow begged. "Look, I'm tired and hungry and thirsty and all over blood and mud, thank you very much, and I'm *not* moving until some of that's remedied, at least. And you don't look like your leg's really all right, either."

"It will take time to mend fully," Blade shrugged. "It cannot be helped, although I fear it will make riding uncomfortable."

"No doubt," Shadow chuckled at the mental picture of Blade sitting on a pillow on her saddle.

"I find nothing so amusing in either my pain or my ruined trousers," Blade said disgustedly.

"They're not ruined," Shadow said, relenting. "If you've got any black leather I can use, I'll mend them when we camp. They need the mud and blood cleaned off anyway, and so do mine, or they'll get stiff and chafe."

"I trust your stitchery is better than your cooking," Blade said distrustfully. "I must, after all, wear these trousers."

"Ha! Travel with a warrior, and mending leather is one thing you can't help but learn," Shadow said ruefully. "Everything from scabbards to breastbands. Not that it isn't a handy skill to have if your clothes suffer as many mishaps as mine seem to do."

"They may suffer one yet," Blade shrugged. "There is still the rest of the river to cross."

Shadow looked out over the river and grimaced. The far bank seemed no nearer than when they had started.

"I thought we'd be most of the way across," she sighed.

"We drifted somewhat downstream, of course," Blade shrugged. "It does not much matter, since the river is carrying us east, which is where we wish to go; but we dare not go much farther downstream, for there will be rapids there, and rocks, and the raft would be beaten to pieces and us with it.''

"Couldn't we stay here on the island tonight?" Shadow suggested. "We'd be in better shape to take it in the morning.''

"And what should we do if it rains again?" Blade mocked. "The river need not rise much more before this island will be gone, and to attempt to cross the river in darkness would be a greater foolishness than even you would dare risk.''

"All right, all right, you know best," Shadow sighed, stepping carefully to the edge of the river to rinse the blood from her hands. "Do you want smoked eel or trail rations?''

Blade looked askance at Shadow and took out a trailbar without another word. Shadow grinned and pulled out a strip of smoked eel to nibble. Blade might never know that Shadow, while no cook, was quite adept at preserving food for the trail.

Blade finished the trailbar disinterestedly, washing it down with wine, then rinsed most of the blood from her thigh.

"Are you ready?" she said impatiently. "We have lost much time. If we wait much longer, the sun will set before we are across.''

"All right," Shadow said reluctantly. She fortified herself with a few hearty swallows of wine, blindfolded the miserable roan, led it and the bay aboard the raft, and helped Blade fasten the daggertooth back into its harness. Then there was only to push the raft back out, the daggertooth swimming strongly to help, and the meager safety of the island receded quickly behind them.

Perhaps they had moved into a swifter channel of the river, or perhaps it was because they were already weary, but Shadow thought the river was moving more swiftly and strongly now. Certainly it was harder, much harder, to control the raft's movement, and even the daggertooth seemed to be having difficulty balking the current. Shadow wondered worriedly how far they were from the rapids Blade had mentioned.

There were more logs, too, and the raft bucked and shuddered incessantly until both of them were drenched by the water splashing over them. Shadow alternated between lending her weight to the rudder oar, and slipping over the logs to calm her half-crazed horses. Then the current became too strong even for that small choice, and she and Blade struggled with the rudder with all their strength, trying to exert at least some small control over the swaying raft. It seemed hours since they had left the island behind.

A huge, multiforked log crashed resoundingly into the side of the raft, and for a moment the platform angled sharply upward. Shadow clung to the rudder oar, feeling her feet leave the slick logs for a moment as the force spun her through the air.

Then she was back on the logs, but only briefly, as the swirling water snapped the oar out of Blade's hands. The thick limb slammed into Shadow and flung her, breathless, into the flood.

This time there was no time to take a breath. She snorted helplessly, swallowing muddy water. Tree limbs and other floating debris buffeted her; out of the corner of her eye she saw the bloated carcass of a deer speed past.

I'll look like that in a bit, she thought.

The water was icy cold, sapping her strength even further, and she could only paddle weakly to stay afloat as best she could. A heavy log thumped her painfully in the ribs, and Shadow seized at it, only to be knocked away as another branch smacked dizzily into the side of her head. Blood ran into her eyes. She opened her mouth to call out and water immediately rushed in.

Something cold and hard was suddenly under her, rising toward the surface. Shadow wrapped her legs around it desperately, and abruptly her head was above water. Wet air rushed into her lungs.

"Stay where you are!" Blade's voice came over the roar of the river. "I cannot leave the rudder to pull you aboard!"

"All right!" Shadow croaked back. Stay where she was? Where was she?

Her head reeling, Shadow wiped water and blood out of her eyes and looked down. She was sitting astride a scaled black back. The daggertooth's back. Shadow laughed, choked, and coughed up water; she choked and laughed again.

Thankfully the shore was not far ahead; the daggertooth's back was painfully knobby and icy cold, and its movements too violent to draw her legs up out of the chilling water.

No one could have been happier than Shadow at the moment when the daggertooth's pushing legs met the bottom of the river; Shadow, however, was too chilled and weak to do more than slide limply from its back and crawl the few feet to land, where she collapsed on the muddy grass.

Blade slogged through the shallow water and pulled the raft up, with the daggertooth's help, onto the bank, tying it to a tree. Daggertooth became dagger. Blade pulled the wretched horses from the raft by main force and tethered them to the same tree. She pulled Shadow's cloak from the saddlebag and threw it over her.

"Stay here," Blade said. "I will find a higher place to camp. We are obviously going no farther today."

Shadow nodded and huddled in her cloak, watching Blade move catlike into the low river scrub. It seemed like hours before she returned astride her demon horse.

"I have found a place," she said. "It is not far, but I think your horses are too shy and you too weak to ride. You will ride with me and we will lead your horses."

"If you like," Shadow said dubiously. She did not want to touch that thing again; horse or daggertooth, the touch of it chilled her with a cold that was not truly physical. She looked at her roan, however, and saw the sense of Blade's argument. Blade had to lift her onto the demon's back, but once there she was able to sit, her arms clasped around Blade's waist.

"Be flattered," Blade said without feeling. "I have allowed no other at my back for some time."

"You have nothing to fear from me," Shadow chuckled tiredly. "Even if I had the inclination, I'm afraid a two-season babe could best me in combat at the moment."

Blade was correct; the campsite was not far, but it was high enough that should the river rise, they would be safe. For once, Shadow sat idle while Blackfell hunted and a disgusted Blade set up camp, this time setting up the tent as well as making a firepit. As soon as there was a fire, Shadow quickly took off her wet clothes, laying them by the fire to dry, and sat down in her blanket as close to the flames as she dared get. She had cleaned the wound on her head and inspected the heavy bruises on her ribs, and felt disinclined to be helpful.

"On the way back," she vowed, "we'll take the Sun Road and sleep comfortably in inns and trail shelters."

"Perhaps you will," Blade shrugged. "I will travel alone."

"You can't be serious," Shadow protested. "Why in the world should the two of us take the risks of riding back to Allanmere alone when we could travel together?"

Blade turned a cold eye to her companion.

"If I do not succeed in killing Baloran," she said, "you would be ill advised to seek my company. Blackfell begins to hunger."

Shadow shuddered, her eyes darting involuntarily to the dagger. "Well, we'll succeed," she said quickly. "So then you won't need to travel alone."

"And you are, of course, assuming that we will both live to return to Allanmere."

"True enough," Shadow said cheerfully, though through chattering teeth. "But if I assume we won't, there's no point in going on, is there?"

"Ah, so now we can add hope to your many other

needs," Blade said indifferently. "What a number of things you require simply to keep you going!"

"Well, you can add greed to the list, if you like," Shadow laughed. "But what keeps you going, if not hope?"

"You may say revenge, if you like," Blade said indifferently. "But the truth is that the alternative to going on is worse."

"Oh." Shadow had no ready answer to that. It occurred to her that even having Blade constantly annoyed with her was preferable to this gloomy mood, and the easiest way to annoy Blade was to ask her a question.

"Among the elves, when we're cold and wet and tired, we sing and dance to warm ourselves," Shadow said reminiscently. "Didn't your folk ever sing and dance?"

"Music," Blade said sourly. "We neither sang nor played. We had never heard music, nor heard of it, and as well. It is only noise to my ears. We had drums, yes, and we danced—"

"What, danced to just drums?" Shadow asked skeptically.

"Or nothing." Blade shrugged. "We danced from here"—tapping her heart—"not here," tapping her ear.

Shadow sniffed dubiously but said nothing, grinning inwardly.

Blade shrugged and drew her dagger.

"Blackfell," she said.

The dagger vanished. In her hands were two small drums, fastened together in the middle. Blade held the drums between her knees. She glanced briefly at Shadow through the fire, then pulled off her gloves.

Shadow's brow wrinkled. There was something odd about Blade's hands, but she could not see clearly through the dancing flames.

Blade struck the drums lightly with her open palms in an odd, irregular rhythm that seemed no rhythm at all until Shadow began to detect a subtle pattern that wound through it. Blade began to vary her strokes, using palms, fingertips, the heels of her hands, and even her knuckles to produce different sounds and patterns. Shadow almost ignored the emergence of the increasingly complex patterns for the spectacle of Blade's hands, now moving so quickly and gracefully that they seemed to be dancing themselves. Blade's face was blank, peaceful.

"Continue," Blade said, startling Shadow. She set the black drums down on the ground, but the intricate rhythms continued. Blade drew on her black gloves again and rose to her feet, drawing two daggers from their sheaths in her boots.

She stepped precisely—toe, pause, then heel—catlike, a slow, stalking tread, but moving her entire body as if one step came from the top of her head and moved down. The knives moved slowly in her hands, then faster, moving as agilely through the black-gloved fingers as if they were but another digit.

Blade wove through the rhythm of the drum, stepping precisely onto each note as it fell to the ground in front of her, pivoting to land in a new pattern, a new rhythm.

Shadow had never seen anything like it. She had seen elvan dances so graceful and beautiful that they brought tears to the eyes. Her own mother, Elia, had been nicknamed Wisp-in-the-Wind for the lightness of her step, so delicate that it seemed it could lift the heart of any watcher to flight.

But this was different. This was not the grace of autumn leaves floating on the wind; this was the grace of a cat stalking its prey. She seemed to fly, but this was not the sweet flight of a songbird; this was the precise and deadly spiral of a hawk. Her daggers glistened in the firelight, her hair and clothes vanishing into the night, her pale skin shocking in the flickering of shadow and light. It was the precise dance of a spider across its glistening web, spiraling ever nearer to its prey.

Like that same prey, Shadow felt herself drawn into the dance like a bird to the snake's hypnotic gaze. The blanket fell forgotten to the ground as Shadow rose, drawn to the dance as inexorably as if the drumbeats were links of a chain pulling her toward the cleared ground around the fire.

Shadow had danced many times before: old dances passed on from mother to child, new dances born from the imaginations of young, hot-passioned elves in the High Circle, joyous improvised celebration dances springing as naturally from feast and festival as flowers sprang from fertile ground after the first warm spring rains. This was something else, a dance of darkness—not the darkness of evil, but perhaps the darkness of secrets—drawn from the hidden places in the spirit, born of passions too complex or perhaps too simple for words, emotions that had no name.

Shadow wove into Blade's dance as one complex pattern of drumbeats wove into another, her skin smoky in the firelight where Blade's was moon-pale, her black hair flickering with red shimmers where Blade's cast back a steel-blue shine. Briefly, they danced closer—close enough that Shadow's fingertips brushed Blade's black-gloved hands and the deadly steel fingers they clasped—then away again, separated by the fire as two verses of a song might be separated by a chorus shared by each.

Cold was gone, weariness was gone, pain was gone. Shadow's skin gleamed in the firelight, her braids unbound, her hair a waving cloak that fell where it would—along the clean line of her back, over her shoulders to veil her nudity, in her face until the wind of her movement swept it clear.

Abruptly Blade dropped the daggers, seized the black drums, and flung them into the fire.

"Stop!" she screamed.

Shadow stumbled and nearly fell into the fire herself, hurriedly seizing her dagger first and then her blanket. She looked wildly around, ready for some enemy to burst forth from the bushes.

The demon rose smoothly from the flames, unharmed, and squatted to the side, unperturbed. Shadow stared, amazed, as Blade stood where she was, staring at Shadow, every muscle taut and trembling, fists clenched so tightly that Shadow thought the stitching in her black gloves must surely give way under the strain. There was an expression on her face Shadow had never seen before—an anger so great, a despair so deep, that Shadow told herself that no enemy could face them more deadly than the one standing before her at that moment.

For a moment Blade stood frozen. Then she stepped outside the circle of firelight into the darkness beyond. Shadow heard only a brief rustling of cloth before Blade returned, wrapped in her cloak. She flung the black trousers at Shadow's feet.

"Mend them," she gritted from between clenched teeth.

Shadow said nothing, only picked up the trousers and reached for her mending kit. Blade sat down across the fire from her, her eyes distant, picking at the food and saying nothing until Shadow returned the trousers. Then, still without a word, she turned and lay down on her pallet, her back to Shadow.

Shadow sighed and ate a few bites of the fish now dry and overcooked, but she was too tired to be hungry. She drank rather more wine than was wise and wearily curled up on her own pallet. She could not have slept more quickly if the hard ground had been the softest of beds.

"Great good gods," Oram murmured. Donya was silent.

Before them was a great pavilion, decorated in red and gold. Panels of scarlet silk blew gently in the spring breeze, apparently untouched by the previous night's rain. Chimes, dangling from the eaves, tinkled musically in the breeze.

A panel of silk moved aside, brushed by a languid hand, and the pavilion's owner stepped regally into view.

Donya was flabbergasted by his youth. Baloran had not changed, if the pictures in the history were true, from the date of the Black Wars. Tall he was, and slender, his skin bronzed gold by the sun; his shoulder-length hair was so golden that it might have been a small sun itself. His eyes were blue as a summer sky, and bright with happiness.

"Fair morn, my lady Donya," he said. His voice was rich

and sweet. "How honored I am that you've journeyed these many miles to greet me."

Donya slowly dismounted, sheathing her sword, and straightened with what dignity she could muster.

"Fair morn, Lord Baloran," Donya said, bowing. "I have come on behalf of High Lord Sharl and High Lady Celene of Allanmere to extend their compliments and to parlay, if you will so allow."

"Nothing would please me more," Baloran smiled. "Allow me to offer you luncheon—food and fire, as the elves would say."

Donya's eyebrows raised slightly; was he unfamiliar with the elvan customs of food and fire, or was his invitation more than slightly suggestive?

"And your men," Baloran continued. "My servants will bring them refreshment. Those that you do not desire to accompany you, of course."

His addendum was so tactfully phrased, his smile so open, that Donya decided that to take any of the guard with her would be nothing more than an insult. Ten men, after all, could do little against a mage of Baloran's might; the gain was not worth the mistrust it signaled.

"My men can wait here," Donya said smoothly, ignoring Oram's cough of warning. "I'd be honored to dine with you."

"The honor, my lady, is mine alone," Baloran said, bowing. He stepped forward to extend his hand; Donya found herself, to her surprise, placing her own hand in it. Baloran's grasp was warm and firm; he raised her hand to his lips, irregardless of the not-too-clean status of that same hand.

They stepped through the curtained archway; Donya felt a brief resistance, then a yielding, as if they had stepped through something thicker than air. She'd known, though, that the mage had to be protecting his pavilion with magic; silk was no barrier to the region's wet and often brutal spring weather.

A feast was already awaiting them on a dark wood table inlaid with silver. Soft music came from some invisible source; sweet-smelling incense burned in decorative urns. Donya was aghast; the food laid out would have fed all fifty of her men amply.

"Were you expecting other guests?" she asked lamely.

Baloran chuckled.

"Ah, my lady, in matters of magic it is often easier to do too much than too little. I learned that during the wars. Do you know, I'd no idea what you might enjoy, so I thought to present you with a variety. Perhaps you and your men might relish some food to take with you when you leave. But I pray that that will not be too soon," he added.

He gestured to a decanter of golden wine, the goblets sitting beside it.

"Please pour, my lady," he said. "I'd not have you think I tried to poison you. I'll take any goblet you choose, and drink first."

The warm humor in his voice made Donya feel foolish, but better embarrassed than dead, she reminded herself sternly. She poured two goblets of the wine, handing one to Baloran. He raised it with a gentle smile in a silent toast, then drank, his eyes sparkling as if they shared a joke. Donya smiled back and sipped exquisite, delicate wine.

Although Blade's slightly softer mood appeared to have remained behind in the swamp, the plains were a welcome relief to Shadow. Here there were sunlight and green things, healthy flowers and plants, and the plentiful scurry of familiar small life. Shadow annoyed Blade further by unconscious bursts of tuneless song, stifled only by another black look from her companion, but her spirits were too high to be so completely subdued. When she was not carving Blade's bow from horseback, her own bow was in use, and when they stopped in the evening, there was no need for Blackfell to hunt, for Shadow had filled her game bag to bursting hours before with the fattest game she could scare up from the grass.

When they camped, Blade looked with some amusement at the quantity of game. "You will be all night cleaning those," she said sourly.

"Well, let your demon help me, as he won't have to hunt," Shadow grinned sheepishly. "Tomorrow night we may be too close to Baloran's place for a campfire, so we may as well feast tonight."

Blade sighed exaggeratedly. "Give me two of the fowl when they are cleaned, and the pot, and what spices you have brought," she said. "A feast, then, you will have."

Shadow grinned again, but to herself, not surprised that Blade made no offer to help clean the game. She set to work on the fowl.

Blade picked through her spices and seasonings, sniffing and tasting, then, to Shadow's surprise, unrolled a pouch of her own containing similar small packets, plus a few leaves, fungi, and tubers she had gathered in the swamp. She dropped bits of this and that into the pot, poured in a hefty measure of wine, and cut up the two fowl neatly, peeling several tubers to go with them. She finished the mixture with a tiny cup of Dragon's Blood.

When she was done she put the lid on the pot, then glanced at the demon, who was helping Shadow pluck feathers from the other fowl.

"Mud," she said.

The demon put down the bird it was plucking and vanished, to Shadow's annoyance—at least it could have finished what it was doing first—but reappeared almost instantly with a large double handful of thick river mud. To Shadow's surprise, it plastered the mud over and around the cooking pot, sealing the crack where the lid met the pot, then placed the pot near the fire to dry. When the mud was dry, it blithely placed the pot into the fire, heaping ashes and coals over the mud-caked surface.

"I don't suppose," Shadow said humbly, "you'd care to

share that technique with a pathetic cook who's willing to learn?''

Blade gave her a mocking glance.

"And what," she asked, "will you wager me for that?''

Shadow shrugged. "If we survive," she said, "I'll think of something. First I'll try it and see if it's worth it." She skewered the last of the game—a rabbit—and handed it to the demon to be set over the fire, then pulled out a dagger to toss.

"You are everlastingly fidgeting with your hands," Blade said annoyedly. "Can you never be still?''

Shadow shrugged, grinning.

"Never could," she apologized. "I'm not used to just sitting. It galls me.''

"You should learn juggling," Blade growled, "and perform in the marketplace.''

"Learn?" Shadow grinned. She pulled out a second knife and added it to the first, then a third.

"I can go to four," she said, "on a good day.''

"Then let us hope," Blade said mildly, "that today is a good day." Abruptly she tossed a dagger to Shadow—the black one.

Reflexively Shadow caught the dagger and worked it in with the other three, her eyes widening as she realized what it was that she juggled. She was risking something more than a cut here if she dropped one or caught it awry!

Grimly she concentrated on the four blades—three bright, one dark—flipping through her hands, coordinating her movements until she was flipping the three metal daggers with one hand and the demonically black one with the other. Without warning, she flipped the black dagger so that it flew, hand over hand, to stick in the ground by Blade's foot. One by one, she caught the other three daggers and sheathed them.

"I think"—she grinned—"it's a good day.''

Donya put down her goblet and stared at the number of empty plates around her puzzledly. How much wine had she drunk, how much food had she eaten? Indeed, how long had she been here eating and drinking with Baloran? She couldn't remember. Surely it had been some time, for the sweet smell of the incense had grown heavy and almost cloying, but sunlight still filtered in brightly through the silk hangings, and the food was still warm and fresh.

"You were telling me of the Eye of Urex," Baloran prompted.

"I—was?" Donya paused, confused. She couldn't remember what she'd been talking about.

"Yes. You came on behalf of the High Lord and Lady of Allanmere to request its return," Baloran smiled. "I would be delighted, my lady, to oblige so charming an envoy; however, I cannot return what I do not have."

"That's impossible," Donya said. It was hard to concentrate. How much wine had she drunk? "You—you have to have it. No one else could."

"My word, my lady, I do not," Baloran said earnestly. "For your sake I am sorry you have journeyed so long to find me to no avail, however delightful I have found your company. I would be glad to help you if I could."

Donya shook her head confusedly. She felt oddly vague and disconnected. Was it only her muzzy head, or were the pavilion and its contents becoming somehow blurred and ill-defined?

"What will you do now, my lady?" Baloran asked, leaning forward. "Will you return to Allanmere with your men?"

"I . . . can't," Donya murmured. "The Council of Churches . . . I have to find it. I'll go—the map, yes. Other places to look."

"The map?" Baloran prompted gently. Donya found herself handing him the rolled leather. He unrolled it, surveying her markings with interest.

"Ah, my lady, how unfortunate," he said. "What am I to do now? My master will not like this."

". . . master?" Donya murmured. Words came hard, too hard.

"Oh, my lady, you will forgive me a small ruse," Baloran laughed. His features were changing, melting away. "My master could not greet you here himself, for he has other guests to greet, but he sent me to welcome you to his lands. I fear, however, you must meet with him himself. Come."

The tall, dark thing that Donya had once thought was Baloran rose, extending one of four hands. Donya numbly clasped the hand, which pulled her to her feet. She followed silently after the creature, able only to look back mutely.

"Oh, do not fear for your men, my lady," the creature said. "I have not been ordered to harm them. Nay, the creatures you met were not sent by my master's orders; they are their own law, being a pack of bandits with whom my master had some unhappy dealings. They will trouble your men no further, for you have come to a land on which they will no longer trespass."

Two of its black hands gestured. A shimmering curtain materialized in the air before them. Through its glistening silver surface, Donya could see another room, a smaller room, built of blocks of white stone.

"Come, my lady," the demon said courteously. "My master awaits."

Donya stepped silently through the curtain.

Early the next morning Shadow began to get a sense of what Celene had meant by "a troubling of the natural forces." The first signs were subtle, noticeable only, perhaps, to someone alert for them—a change not so much noticeable to the eye as to the spirit. Perhaps the wind smelled slightly odd, or the sky was a slightly different shade; perhaps it was the song of the birds that seemed to have altered somehow. Perhaps it was only a vague sense of unease, an indefinable feeling that something was awry, akin to the prickling Shadow felt at the back of her neck if someone was watching her.

"Stop looking over your shoulder like that," Blade said irritably.

"I feel like someone's watching me," Shadow said nervously.

"No one is watching you. Now stop jumping about."

"How do you know?" Shadow said. "The back of my neck's prickling. How do you know Baloran isn't watching us this instant through a crystal ball or something?"

"He is not."

"How do you know that?" Shadow insisted.

Blade sighed annoyedly. "Because Blackfell shields me from such detection, and, by proximity, you as well. That is his particular ability, and undoubtedly why Baloran summoned him to begin with. It was likely quite handy during the wars."

Shadow pulled her horse to a halt, staring at Blade amazedly. "Why didn't you tell me that before?" she demanded.

"And why should I have?" Blade retorted. "It is no business of yours."

"We're walking into a mage's lair and you don't think it's my business?" Shadow demanded.

"I did not force you into this," Blade said pointedly. "As I recall, you went to some pains to enlist *me*. There was no discussion of an exchange of our respective secrets. You already know more of me than I like. I tell you now only so that you do not make the rest of this journey a misery jumping about like a mouse in a snake pit."

Shadow raised an eyebrow. "Anything else you'd like to tell me now, while you're at it?"

Blade's eyes were icy. "There is nothing I would like to tell you, including many things you already know. Now let me be."

Shadow sighed unhappily, not reassured. Mages might well be daunted by such things; she certainly hoped so.

Elves, though, wouldn't rely on plain magic; elves would have birds watching from the sky or small scurrying things from the grass. Unless Blackfell could make them all invisible—Shadow had heard of such things—nothing was hiding them from beast-eyes.

"Mages do not use animals," Blade said from beside her.

Shadow jumped. "Is thought-reading among your many unlisted abilities?" she asked accusingly.

Blade chuckled coldly. "You have been staring askance at every bird overhead and every field mouse underfoot," she said. "I remember what you told me of the elves. Beasts dislike magic; they are shy of it. That is why mages tamper with them, breed them into chancy things to serve them."

Blade shrugged. "But there is more than that. You have felt it in the air. Proximity to such powerful magic changes things over time—the plants, the animals. Over time they become stranger and stranger as the residues of magic work on them."

"You mean like city rats get fatter than woods rats?" Shadow asked, frowning.

"No." Blade was silent for a moment. "You spoke of the elves and how many of them were barren, and you said that since the tribes have been mixing together, more children are born; is that not so?"

"Yes," Shadow said, puzzled. "There aren't as many barren now as there used to be. There aren't as many short elves now, either, nor as many born gifted with beast-speaking or other gifts. But what's that got to do with magic?"

"It is much the same thing," Blade said impatiently. "In the case of the elves, the thing that changed them was the blending of the tribes, the breeding of members of one tribe with another. With magic, magic is the thing which changes them. The first animals are changed just a bit, you see, perhaps not enough to notice, by the magic that creeps into them. But then those changed offspring breed with other changed offspring, who are in turn changed even more, do you see, until many generations, many years later, you have something truly changed."

"It's been centuries," Shadow protested, "and the elves haven't changed all that much."

"Oh, you insist on not understanding," Blade growled. "An elf breeds only a time or two in a century, you said so; but animals breed frequently and bear many. Thus they change the faster."

"You don't need to get so angry," Shadow said mildly. "I'm sure I'm no authority on mages. Fortune favor me, the less I know about them the better, I say, except for whatever I need to learn to rob one!"

Blade looked at her sideways, then chuckled grudgingly. "What an odd creature you are," she said. "I doubt Baloran can have bred anything so strange as you!"

"Yes," Shadow laughed. "I guess I am strange, at that. Ask anyone who knows me!"

Within a few hours, however, Shadow might have disputed Blade's assessment of Baloran's odd creatures. As they rode, the strange feeling of alienness increased.

More noticeable signs of Baloran's presence could be seen. The vegetation was . . . different. The tall prairie grasses grew in odd off-shades—some tinged with blue or red or purple. Interspersed with the more common prairie grasses and flowers grew more unusual foliage—odd vines and creepers the like of which Shadow had never seen, some beautiful, some ugly, some merely unusual.

Then there were the animals. They were few and shy, but Shadow caught glimpses from time to time of disturbing inhabitants of the prairie—a white weasel who seemed to have too many legs; a hawk with grasping paws instead of talons; a rabbit splotched with purple and gold; a lizard who, startled, unfurled batlike wings; a fleet deerlike creature with shimmering scales instead of fur.

"Just as well we have so much food put up," Shadow commented after the last sighting. "I don't know as I'd feel smart hunting here."

Blade shook her head. "Nor would I feel wise in eating anything you might shoot," she agreed. "Best that we avoid both hunting and fires; what either might draw to us, I do not wish to know."

"We should camp soon," Shadow said. "If we're that close to Baloran's keep, we should camp while we're still far enough out of sight."

Blade nodded. "I would send Blackfell to scout the distance," she said, "but I do not want him far from my side here. I think we should scout carefully on foot to see how far we are, then set a camp."

"Smart," Shadow nodded. She pointed north at what appeared to be a small streambed, where a low line of trees and scrub broke the smooth prairie. "How about there? The trees will give us some shelter if it rains, and we won't be so visible."

Blade nodded absently, her eyes never leaving the horizon.

"Very well; but we will camp north of Baloran's place. I would not be downstream of him and his."

Using the stream for cover, Shadow and Blade moved northeast, watching carefully.

"Stay low," Blade said as they continued northeast through the prairie grass.

"Bet on it," Shadow muttered sarcastically. The grass was mostly taller than she, and she was making an all-too-close inspection of the bizarre foliage at its base. There were pink, fleshy-looking tendrils that seemed to move slightly, and it was easy to imagine them reaching for her, stretching out fingerlike to grasp at her. She kicked them away and hurried after Blade.

Blade stopped so quickly that Shadow nearly ran into her back. Blade crossly motioned her to silence, pointing ahead of them. Shadow looked, and her jaw dropped.

There was a castle sitting in the middle of the prairie, a fortress built out of stone as white as bone. It was surrounded by a ditch filled with water—not precisely a moat, but wide enough that a small bridge crossed it.

"Illusion?" Shadow murmured to Blade. Blade drew her black dagger, glanced at it, and shook her head.

"Well, what then?" Shadow demanded. "How many people can he have in there and nobody know where it is?"

"There are no people there," Blade whispered. "Only Baloran and the things he creates there or summons to him."

"Oh, thank you," Shadow murmured back. "*That* reassures me. Come on, it must have taken hundreds of men to build that castle."

"No men built that castle," Blade whispered back. "In fact I much doubt whether it was built at all. When Baloran lived near Allanmere, he had a small castle of his own. If that is not the same castle, it is identical."

Shadow glanced at her companion, wondering if Blade was joking, but Blade was staring at the castle, her face set in concentration.

"Are you there, mage?" Blade whispered softly, so softly Shadow almost did not hear. "Are you afraid? Fear me, Baloran, for I am coming for you and this time it is my game, not yours."

Shadow looked away and shivered. She didn't know which was more frightening—having Baloran for an enemy or Blade for an ally.

"We will camp," Blade said at last. "I have seen enough."

They circled around to the north, widely skirting the area of the castle, and camped upstream of it. Once settled, they dined quietly on the smoked fish and meat Shadow had prepared. Blade made no admission that the food was better than she had expected, but she ate without complaint, and that was enough for Shadow, who was in no mood for bantering.

When she was finished, there was still light enough, so she wandered a few yards downstream until she found the right bathing spot—a quiet place with a gently sloping sandy bottom, and where the water was clear. She hung her clothes over a bush and unbound her long braids, wading only far enough into the cool water to a point where she could sit comfortably on the sandy floor to wash.

It felt as though she had a week's accumulated swamp muck to wash off her hair and skin, although logic told her that her many rain wettings and her swim in the river must have washed away a good deal of it. Still, there was a great deal of difference between a couple of rinsings in muddy water and a good scrub in a clean stream with the soap she'd brought wishfully with her.

Fortune, what she'd give for a nice, soft, warm bed, she thought, shivering a little in the chill water, a *hot* bath and a handsome bathboy to go with it, a hot supper in a tavern somewhere with lots and lots of wine, a few friendly fellows with dice in their hands and money in their pockets, and maybe a nice brawny fellow, smelling of wine and leather, who'd care to come to her room for gaming of a different sort.

"I knew that Fortune-be-damned Guild would be more trouble than it was worth," she grumbled, rubbing soap into her hair and knuckling the foam out of her eyes. "I *knew* it'd be nothing but a headache. I didn't know it'd also be a backache, and a neckache, and a couple of legaches, and especially a buttache. Whatever human got the stupid idea of domesticating those Fortune-be-damned moving mountains should have also invented some comfortable way for people to sit on them for hours at a time!

"Next time," Shadow vowed, "I'm bringing six horses and a wagon no matter what. Next time I'm going to hire a dozen hefty bodyguards. Next time I'm going to bring ten barrels of wine. Fortune favor me, next time I'm going to *let* Donya storm the damned castle and get her fool self killed!"

Shadow sighed exaggeratedly and dunked her hair underwater, scrubbing vigorously at the soap. When she surfaced, sputtering and pushing the wet hair out of her eyes, she was amazed to see Blade sitting on the bank, looking bored.

"How long have you been sitting there?" Shadow demanded.

Blade shrugged. "Since you went into the water," she said. "As I told you, Blackfell is my defense against Baloran's mage-sight, and I am yours. Therefore we must not be separated. Are you going to tell me now I have violated your modesty?" she added mockingly.

"No, just my privacy," Shadow said annoyedly. "You might have said something, you know, to let me know you were there."

Blade shrugged again. "What difference does it make? You did not, after all, have your dozen bodyguards here."

Shadow scowled but decided argument was futile. "If you want a bath," she said, "I've got some soap."

Blade raised one eyebrow and smiled, a smile that never reached her eyes. "Thank you, but I prefer my baths heated," she said. "And I do not find it wise to discard clothes and weapons so short a distance from my enemy's lair."

"I suppose you're right," Shadow sighed. She stood up, wrung the water out of her hair as best she could, and slogged toward shore. "But if I'm going to my death, I'm not going to it *dirty*."

"Well, I do not want to go to my death thirsty," Blade declared. "So let us go back to camp, if you will, and attend to my thirst as thoroughly as you have attended to your cleanliness."

"Now, that I can agree with," Shadow said, pleased. She eyed her clothes critically, decided that their river dunking had rendered them clean enough to suffice, and put them back on.

Back at the camp, Blade set out wine and Dragon's Blood while Shadow combed the snarls out of her wet hair and rebraided it. That task also took rather more time than Blade would have liked.

"Such long hair cannot but be a hindrance," Blade commented idly. "It would afford a handy grasp in combat, and an enemy could well throttle you with your own hair. An expensive vanity."

Shadow chuckled. "Do you know, I'd never thought of my hair as a combat liability," she grinned. "Inconvenient at times, yes. But it's handy in dealing with other elves—special treatment, respect, sometimes the odd edge in a bargain. When I was young, you know, elves marked their age by the length of their hair, age being the only kind of status we had. These days it's still respected, more out of habit, I guess, than anything else, but I see the younger elves cutting their hair, especially the elves who spend their time in town or live there. A couple of centuries from now, I doubt the title of Matriarch is going to mean anything at all here." Shadow shrugged ruefully. "I guess I'm just an old-fashioned girl." She secured the last loop of her braid with a gold pin. "Besides, it gives me a place to hang all my Guild tokens."

"Well, stop preening and start drinking," Blade said, handing her a cup of wine. "You were the one wishing for ten barrelsful."

"Aye, and I could drink the lot, bet on it," Shadow grinned. "Since this may be our last night alive, how about some dreamweed to go with the liquor?"

"Why not?" Blade said. "If you have the dreamweed."

"Indeed I have," Shadow grinned, pulling a pouch out of her saddlebags. "Better than my forest-patrol friends, but it would've been rude to say so. I'm fortunate enough to be friends with the best dreamweed merchants in Allanmere."

"Argent and Elaria," Blade nodded. "I remember."

"Oh, that's right." Shadow filled the pipe and lit it, and took an experimental puff. "Mmmm."

Blade took the pipe, drew on it, then nodded. "Better," she agreed absently. She pulled out her tiny cups and poured Dragon's Blood, handing one cup to Shadow.

"I'll give you this, you're either very brave or very

foolish,'' Shadow chuckled. "I've seen humans walk off roofs from a few puffs of dreamweed that potent, and *I've* almost walked off a few roofs myself with a taste or two of that Dragon's Blood. You may yet save Baloran some trouble, unless your demon protects you from drunkenness and pipe-dreams, too.''

Blade gave her a narrow look but said nothing, simply quaffing her Dragon's Blood and reaching again for the pipe.

"I have, of course,'' Blade said, "no reason to believe that this castle is identical to the one I entered so many years ago; however, to the eye, I would say that it is. I have drawn a diagram of the interior as I remember it, and marked what defenses I know of—which knowledge, of course, is most likely entirely useless.''

She spread out the skin on the ground, pausing between puffs on the pipe.

"The lowest level, below the ground, is the cellars,'' Blade said, pointing. "I had no occasion to visit those. The ground-level rooms are such rooms as one might expect to find—kitchens, storage rooms, a dining room—''

"You said there was no one there but him,'' Shadow argued, taking the pipe.

"I said he had no human servants,'' Blade corrected. "When he lived near Allanmere I know not what or who cooked his meals and washed his clothes. As to the dining hall, however, I have it that he infrequently invited other mages and scholars to dine.''

"Go on,'' Shadow said. "What's above the ground level?''

"The second level contains his bedroom and his work-rooms and laboratories,'' Blade said. She tapped one of the smaller rooms. "It was in this one I found the dagger. It was indeed well protected.''

"The room or the dagger?'' Shadow asked.

"Both.''

"Then he'll likely have the gem under similar protections," Shadow mused. "Probably in the same room."

"Unless he has use for it in his work," Blade cautioned.

"Okay, okay," Shadow nodded. "But at least we know that the second floor is where we're most likely to find it, and Baloran."

"I will grant you that," Blade agreed. "He sleeps seldom and eats even less."

Two pipes, half a skin of wine, and some unknown quantity of Dragon's Blood later, Shadow surrendered, waving away the pipe when Blade would have handed it back to her.

"No more, no more," Shadow said, giggling helplessly. "Do you know, the last time I had this much dreamweed and wine, I talked to Fortune herself?"

"I do not doubt it," Blade said with a sneer. She swallowed another cup of Dragon's Blood. "Best you stop, then, for what more can there be after a goddess?"

"How true, how true." Shadow laughed again. "Fortune favor me, don't you *ever* get drunk? Donya once told me I had the best head for liquor and dreamweed she'd ever seen, but you make me look like some cocky young lordling having his first taste of elvan wine."

Blade shrugged.

"Wine to me is nothing but a taste in my mouth. Dragon's Blood alone seems to affect me somewhat, and then only if I drink much of it. Dreamweed is much the same. At this moment I am as intoxicated as I have ever been, I suppose."

Shadow shook her head pityingly.

"Too bad," she said. "I love to overindulge now and then, especially—"

"Yes, when you have a warm bed and a hairy man awaiting," Blade sighed. "How monotonous your pleasures are."

"Only if the man's no good," Shadow giggled.

Blade was silent for a long moment, so long that Shadow, chuckling to herself at her own wit, began to doze.

"Shadow."

Something about Blade's tone cleared some of the fog from Shadow's head, and she sat up. "What?"

Blade had the black dagger out, tracing its tip idly in the dust. She was silent again a long moment before she looked directly into Shadow's eyes.

"We have no bargain for this journey," she said at last. "There are no debts between us. Yet we have shared road and camp and I have trusted you at my back. I would—" she paused, grimacing as if the words came hard. "I would ask a thing of you, and if you will agree to give it, I will owe you a debt which I will one day repay, if I can."

Surprise penetrated even the fog of dreamweed and liquor. What in the *world* might Blade want of her?

"What is it?" Shadow asked.

"If I am slain—" Blade glanced away again, then back. "If I am slain, you know what will become of me. Of my soul. If I were bound to Baloran as Blackfell has been bound to me these many years—" She hesitated again.

"Then you'd better not get killed," Shadow warned. "I couldn't do much against Baloran alone, you know, if you did. Especially if you were working for him then."

Blade nodded absently. "I have no desire for that," she said. "But I ask you to promise me this—if I die, kill Baloran if you can. Only if you can. If you cannot, see that he does not take the dagger. You are safe if you do not touch it yourself. Then give it to some human—anyone you wish—and kill him, or have him killed immediately. This I ask of you."

Shadow was silent for a long moment, thinking that perhaps this was no decision to be made on a headful of wine and dreamweed. She remembered Spirit Lake, and the river, and the sight of Blade dancing, black and silver, in the moonlight.

"All right," she said. "By the Mother Forest, I'll do it,

if I can. I'll do what you ask. Unless it would mean getting me killed," she added quickly.

Blade nodded, her eyes never leaving Shadow's.

"Then, for your promise I owe you a debt," Blade said quietly. "If I am able, it will be repaid."

Shadow nodded back and extended her hand. After a moment, Blade took it briefly, then released it as if she found the touch embarrassing. She turned away hurriedly and reached for the half-empty flask of Dragon's Blood and, to Shadow's utter amazement, swigged from it as if it were a wineskin. She shuddered briefly, but swallowed.

"Fortune favor me," Shadow said in awe. "Who cares what Baloran does—you're going to kill *yourself*."

"No," Blade said. "Tomorrow I will have revenge, if nothing else. That is something that is worth living for."

"Well, it's not worth dying for," Shadow said. "So in the interest of staying alive, I'd like to know if you've got any good ideas on how to get into that place."

Blade nodded. "You will not like it," she said.

"I don't doubt that," Shadow grimaced. "I don't like the whole thing."

"I will have to observe the castle further," Blade said, "but it looks to me as if this very stream by which we have camped feeds the ditch around Baloran's castle. If that is so, it is most likely that there will be a place where this water enters the castle to supply him water, and a place where it exits to carry out waste. These conduits cannot be heavily protected, or the waste could not be carried out."

"Now, wait a minute," Shadow said unhappily. "You can't mean—you mean *swim* in through wherever the water goes in?"

"Yes."

"Now I know that Dragon's Blood has gone to your head," Shadow said, shaking her head. "Blade, as you've probably guessed, my swimming skills are exceeded only by my talent at singing and my fondness for celibacy."

Blade shrugged.

"Then perhaps you can give me a better idea. Doubtless you have robbed many a mage in your time, although I doubt if you have robbed one so powerful as Baloran. You do, after all, have that infamous bracelet. What do you propose?"

"I don't know yet," Shadow sighed, stalling. "Look, I'm drunk and not thinking. We can hardly try to get in tomorrow while it's full daylight. We'll watch the place, and maybe I'll get some ideas then. All right?"

Blade nodded.

"There is no reason not to do as you say," she said. "As you said, there is no wisdom in walking into his lair in full daylight. We have no way to know if he is even there. I would prefer to observe the castle for several days if that were possible."

"So would I, but we don't have the luxury of that much time," Shadow said. "In a few days Donya and her guardsmen will be riding up to his door, and that ends any chance we'll have of surprising him."

"That is another possibility."

"What?" Shadow raised her eyebrows. "What are you talking about?"

Blade shrugged. "The Lady Donya and her guards. They would make an admirable distraction. We could likely slip in unnoticed, and it would be much easier to deal with Baloran when he must divide his attention between the lady and her force and us."

Shadow shook her head firmly. "Oh, no," she said. "Not that. We agreed to be in and out before Donya ever gets here, and I'm serious about that, Blade. Donya's my friend, and I'm not going to use her as bait. She could get killed."

"I am not concerned," Blade said indifferently, "about the Lady Donya."

"Well, I am," Shadow said adamantly. "Besides, you know, there's always the chance she'll kill Baloran herself."

"I doubt that," Blade said with a half smile.

"So do I, but that's not the point," Shadow said. "We agreed to take care of this without involving Donya and her guard, and we're not going to involve them, or all our agreements are off. *All* of them."

Blade looked at Shadow narrowly, but nodded.

"Very well," she said. "Do not believe you have bent me to your will, for you have not; but Blackfell, and therefore I, cannot afford to wait. And it is, of course, entirely possible that the Lady Donya will never arrive at all, having gotten herself and her guard killed elsewhere. Then, too, on the tiny chance that the lady should survive, I would prefer to avoid official entanglements."

"There is that"—Shadow laughed—"since we're contemplating the robbery and murder of one of Allanmere's war heroes."

Blade gave a small smile. "Aye," she said. "Indeed we are."

"Are we agreed, then?" Shadow asked. "We'll observe tomorrow, and if possible, go in tomorrow night?"

Blade took a second deep draught directly from the flask of Dragon's Blood, shivering again as it went down.

"Aye," she said. "We are agreed."

SEVEN ═══════

"Watch again," Shadow said, pointing. "There."

A small winged creature—not a bird, not with those leathery blue wings—circled the castle, spiraling in closer. Abruptly it stalled in the air, dropping several feet before it recovered and veered sharply away.

"Hit something," Shadow said. "Any idea what?"

Blade nodded slowly.

"An invisible barrier," she said. "Such things are known to mages, but they are a great feat, a great drain of power. He used no such wall when he lived near Allanmere. He has grown in his might, grown greatly, or I am much mistaken."

"Maybe it's not his might," Shadow said.

Blade looked over at her questioningly.

"Well, he obviously specializes in summoning up demons and the like," Shadow reasoned. "Maybe something he summoned up is powering that barricade. Or maybe it's something he got during the wars, you know, something he stole that he just didn't bother using before you got through his other defenses. What I mean is, we don't dare assume that he's putting his energy or concentration into that barrier, that that's any drain on him, see?"

"Yes," Blade said after a moment. "You are correct, of course. Nevertheless there are some assumptions we can make."

121

"Oh?"

"That the barrier is not complete," Blade said impatiently. "It allows in the air, or Baloran could not breathe; it allows in the water, or the ditch would be empty or at least stagnant."

"Oh, no," Shadow groaned. "Not back to the water again."

Blade shrugged. "The barrier may not surround the castle totally," she said. "Perhaps it does not extend into the ground; we could dig under it, a project necessitating some time in the open where we could be observed. Perhaps it does not totally cover the top; we could fly over it, a project necessitating that we grow wings. Neither of those solutions, however, gains us entry into the castle itself."

"Not a problem," Shadow said, tapping the bracelet on her wrist. "That I *know* I can handle."

"And of course while we are flying over his wall or digging under it, and opening his doors with powerful magic, Baloran will be quietly sitting in his rooms ignoring the whole thing." Blade shook her head. "No. I think the water is our only chance. We will test it first, of course."

Shadow nodded reluctant agreement.

They crept quietly back to the camp. Shadow picked up a branch and dropped it into the river, watching as it floated toward the castle.

"Can Blackfell follow it?" Shadow asked. "I'm not sure we could see it in the ditch from so far away."

"As long as the ditch is not too shallow," Blade said. "But if it is that shallow, it will be of no use to us, either."

Shadow nodded, secretly hoping that the ditch was much shallower than it looked as the daggertooth waddled into the stream. At this point the rain-swollen stream was certainly deep enough; the daggertooth vanished quickly.

Shadow and Blade returned to their vantage point in the grass, not really hoping to see anything of the branch or the daggertooth, but in case either provoked any kind of response from the castle.

They waited. A few more flying things hit the invisible barrier; Shadow and Blade were able to place it at about twenty paces from the castle, just past the ditch.

There were other disturbing signs—skeletons in various states of decay. As far as Shadow could see they were all beast skeletons of different types, none human, but that was little reassurance. Some appeared charred; in some, the bones were flung far apart, as if they had exploded.

"Have you seen those?" Shadow asked, pointing to the skeletons.

Blade nodded. "I knew Baloran would have many such protections," she said with a shrug. "I am glad to see it."

"Well, I'm not," Shadow scowled. "I've got some extract of moly here, but I don't have a cask of the stuff. It's Fortune-be-damned expensive, you know, and hard to get. What's going to protect both of us from all of his magical traps?"

"Our wits"—Blade shrugged—"and your blasted luck. We are fortunate. If his protections are so thorough outside, the chances are good that they will be less thorough within. We will bypass whatever outer defenses he has in the water."

"And if he has defenses in the water?" Shadow pressed. "I can't even swim. Do you expect me to wrestle dragons, too?"

"If there are defenses in the water, Blackfell will find them," Blade murmured. "If he must, he will leave the water and return in another form. I do not wish him to change form otherwise, for it might attract attention from the castle. And as for your endless reminders that you cannot swim, Blackfell will pull you through the water. You will have only to hold your breath for a time, lest we be seen."

"Oh, that's all?" Shadow said sarcastically. "I'll wait to hear what Blackfell finds out, thank you."

"You need not wait," came the cold, rather breathy voice

of the demon, and Shadow turned to see it climb from the water. It glanced at Blade, who nodded, and squatted in the sand to draw with a stick.

"The ditch is narrow but quite deep," the demon hissed, drawing the moat and the castle. "The water enters through a grate on the north side and exits similarly to the south. The grates are half a man-height square and are wholly underwater."

"And what is in the water?" Blade asked.

"Small life," the demon said. "Nothing of consequence. But I could not pass the grate. It was sealed by a magical force."

"Well, that's that," Shadow said cheerfully. "We're blocked out."

"Then we have three choices," Blade said serenely. "First, we can give up and go back to Allanmere and leave your highborn friend to take care of the situation. Second, we can walk up to Baloran's front door and knock and demand that he let us in. Third, we can go by water anyway and open that magically barred grate with your infamous bracelet. The choice, my dear Guildmistress, is utterly yours."

"Fortune favor me," Shadow sighed dismally. "So how big did you say this grate was?"

In the end they formed a kind of flotilla: Blade with her necessities tied to her belt in a waterproof skin; a highly nervous Shadow similarly laden; and an eight-foot daggertooth with eight bladders filled with air tied to various parts of its body.

"That's not much air," Shadow said dubiously.

Blade shrugged.

"Any more and he will float. Most of the air is for you. I can go long without air."

"You swim a lot?" Shadow asked curiously. She couldn't imagine Blade swimming.

"Something of that nature." Blade inspected the arrangement again. "Hold to the ropes, not to his tail, or you will be knocked silly."

"I don't like this at all," Shadow said for the dozenth time. She waded slowly into the water, giving one of the ropes an experimental jerk.

"That hardly matters," Blade said wryly, following the daggertooth into deeper water. "He will travel at the surface for a time, but be ready when he dives. He is unlikely to warn you."

Shadow grimaced when she felt her feet leave the bottom, but true to Blade's word, the daggertooth swam close to the surface at first, pushing them downstream at a furious rate with the powerful strokes of its tail.

Clinging desperately to the rope, Shadow spluttered miserably as water foamed into her face. The bank was moving past too swiftly, almost as quickly as if she were on a horse at a full gallop.

Abruptly the daggertooth dove. Shadow had just enough time to take a deep breath before the water smacked her in the face and the world disappeared into swirling brown and green. Up her nose, in her eyes, flowing into her ears until she could hear nothing but her own blood pounding—

Shadow groped along the rope until she reached one of the tied bladders and worked it loose. Then she panicked for a moment—for all their planning, Shadow had not anticipated how difficult it would be to untie the opening to one of the bladders while simultaneously holding on to a rope tied around a fast-moving daggertooth. She hooked one arm through the rope and pulled her dagger, sawing at the leather ties until they reluctantly gave way. Blowing out the rest of the stale air in her lungs, she pulled the opening of the bladder to her lips and gasped in the good clean air. She clenched the bladder shut on the remaining air and counted the beats of her heart, trying to ignore the rushing water.

Something struck her leg, a hot, sharp pain, then another— wood, stumps in the river? Shadow tried to pull her legs in, but there was another blow, close to her hip.

Abruptly the daggertooth slowed and stopped. Shadow took the remaining breath in her bladder and let it go, then opened her eyes. There was, indeed, a grate in the water, just in front of the daggertooth. Blade was there, holding to the castle stones and looking back at her.

Shadow reached toward the grating rather dubiously; her fingers came up short a few inches from the metal. Now, what in the world did Blade think she was going to do about that?

Shadow shrugged and reached for another bladder, pulling it loose. It was more awkward than ever, trying to manage the bladder, hold on to the rope, and still keep her left hand free to extend toward the grate. She touched the invisible barrier there, put the opening of the bladder over her mouth, and released the word into its depths:

"Aufrhyr."

There was nothing under her reaching hand to see, but abruptly there was nothing there to touch, either. Then her hand was grasping the bars of the grate and Blade's hands were there, too, prying strongly with the iron bar she had brought. The grate itself, bereft of its magical protection, was nothing; it came easily away.

There was no room for them to swim with the daggertooth through the opening; Shadow took two bladders and held them tightly, grasped the tow rope Blade had tied, and let the daggertooth pull them.

The conduit was far too narrow for comfort, and how long it might be was anyone's guess. Shadow banged and scraped painfully against the top, bottom, and sides of the conduit; Blade, whose tow rope was purposefully shorter than hers, seemed to delight in kicking her in the face. It seemed almost impossible to maneuver a bladder around to where she could reach it, cut the binding cord, and get it to her mouth and nose where she could take a breath, all the while holding tightly to the tow rope as she knocked against algae-coated stone blocks.

Surely the castle couldn't be so long! It seemed twice as

long as the distance from the camp. She reached for another bladder, only to realize dismally that she had used both of them already.

Fortune favor me, I'm going to drown in a mage's sewer.

Abruptly there was a light overhead and Blade's feet were, thankfully, withdrawn from her face. Shadow kicked her way upward, pulling hard on the tow rope, and suddenly she was breathing real air—dank, musty air, but air nonetheless. Shadow sputtered and choked out what seemed like a gallon of water, then grabbed about frantically for support. One of Blade's black-gloved hands clasped hers, and she seized it gratefully, once more marveling at Blade's strength as she was pulled out of the water to collapse on the cold stone, knuckling dirty water out of her eyes.

They were in a small, closed room whose only features were a few barrels, a bucket, and the open length of the conduit they had emerged from. The room was dimly lit by two glowing globes mounted midway up the walls; Shadow remembered something similar from Celene's workroom. It didn't take much to light the smooth, odd white stone.

"Where are we?" she choked.

"I hardly know," Blade said contemptuously. "One of the cellars, most likely. Have you your tinderbox?"

Shadow fumbled it out of her pack, thankful that the fat-and-wax waterproofing had held. She handed the box to Blade.

"Do you really think we should light a torch in here?" she murmured.

"Probably not," Blade said, striking flint and steel. "But before we go farther, best we be rid of your passengers."

"Passengers?" Shadow asked.

Blade gestured, and Shadow glanced down at her legs. Three long, dark things, glistening with slime, had attached themselves to her legs. Small rivulets of blood trickled out from under the places where they had joined to her skin. The creatures were already swollen with stolen blood.

Shadow cried out with disgust, beating frantically at the ugly things to no effect.

"Blackfell," Blade said, sounding bored. The demon seized Shadow's wrists, holding her hands tightly despite her struggles.

"Really," Blade said sarcastically, pulling a candle from her sealed pack and lighting it. "Such fuss over a few leeches. Be still, or you will be burned."

"I *hate* leeches," Shadow choked, pulling desperately at Blackfell's grip.

"Well, these are large ones, to be sure," Blade chuckled coldly, applying the candle flame to the first black leech. It released its hold reluctantly. "No doubt something Baloran bred to inhabit the ditch, and neither large enough nor dangerous enough to attract Blackfell's attention."

"I see *you* didn't get any of them," Shadow growled.

She had stopped struggling, but she looked away while Blade treated the other two leeches to a taste of fire. When they fell away and Blackfell released her, she pulled out a bottle of wine with trembling hands to wash the circular wounds, then drained the bottle—something of a mistake, for the loss of blood was not small to an elf of her slight stature, and it combined with the wine and fear to make her dizzy.

"Come," Blade said impatiently, sheathing the black dagger. "The longer we remain in one place, the more likely we are to be discovered."

"And the sooner we're out of here, the more likely we are to stay alive," Shadow agreed. "Can Blackfell scout for us?"

Blade shook her head. "Best not," she said. "He is a magical presence so strong that Baloran might notice the disturbance. As a dagger he is less noticeable; and besides, I want the weapon to hand."

"Let's go, then," Shadow shrugged.

The plain wooden door swung open with a creak that grated on Shadow's nerves, showing them an empty, stone-floored hallway bordered by other similar doors. There was no one about, but Shadow could hear footsteps from the top of the stairway at the other end of the hall.

"Someone's coming," Shadow hissed. Blade nodded, and they stepped quickly back into the room, leaving the door open just a crack to look out. The footsteps began to descend the stairs, they paused, then continued.

When Blade had said that Baloran had no human servants, she'd had no idea what to expect, but it was not what came walking down the steps to the cellar.

To begin with, it was red—red as blood. It was humanoid in form in that it had two arms and two legs and a head, but it was reed-slender like the most delicate of elves, and there seemed to be too many digits on its thin hands and feet. It was wearing nothing, but its uniformly bloodred body was utterly sexless. It had no hair and no face—the smooth, empty blankness on the front of its head was broken only by two eye-shaped pits.

"Wha—" Shadow started to whisper, but Blade's gloved hand tightened over her mouth.

The odd creature moved smoothly down the hall and opened one of the other doors. Its movements were more unusual than its looks—its limbs articulated oddly, and it moved in a sinuous glide.

"Be silent," Blade breathed into Shadow's ear almost too low to be heard.

The creature emerged from the storeroom carrying a large ham and returned up the stairs as deliberately as it had come.

"What in Fortune's name was that?" Shadow murmured when it was gone.

"An homunculus," Blade told her. "A magical creature partly made and partly summoned. Despite its appearance, its senses are quite acute, and there may well be others."

"Are they dangerous?" Shadow asked.

"Not as dangerous," Blade said grimly, "as I."

"I believe that," Shadow murmured to herself.

They slipped out the door, closing it behind them as quietly as the creaky hinges would allow. The hallway was also lit at regular intervals by the globes, and Shadow wondered to herself, keeping a sort of tally. There was the barrier; that was one thing, and the separate barrier on the grate was another. Then there was the homunculus, and then there were the globes. What other magic was Baloran capable of, and what other possible drains on his powers might there be?

The stone stairs were empty, and Blade started forward, but Shadow put out an arm to bar her.

"What?" Blade whispered.

"I don't know." Shadow squatted on her heels, staring at the stairs.

The homunculus had stepped down—yes, five stairs, then a pause, then nine steps. Something on the fifth stair, then; but was there a trap on the fifth stair to be bypassed, or a trigger to keep a trap at another point from being set off?

"Hurry," Blade murmured.

" 'Hurry now, worry later,' " Shadow said, quoting the old thieves' proverb. Now, where had the homunculus emerged from the staircase? Right, *not* at the center, but to the left side, almost at the wall.

Keeping carefully to the left and motioning Blade to stay back, Shadow placed one careful foot on the lowest step, slowly increasing the weight on it. Nothing happened. She stepped up again, then again, then—

—wait a minute; there were *fifteen* steps! That means—

"Okay," Shadow whispered. "Stay left and follow me."

Blade was almost soundless behind her; no one without an elf's preternatural hearing would have heard her. Shadow continued upward, testing each step before trusting it with her weight. She carefully stepped over the sixth step, glancing back to make sure Blade did the same. She skipped up the rest of the steps to the top, flattening herself against the wall, all senses alert, to peer out a crack in the door.

So far the layout held true to the diagram Blade had

drawn. There was the corridor Blade had drawn, with the doors to the kitchen, the scullery, the pantry, the dining hall. One of the doors was opening—

Shadow cursed to herself, prepared to bolt back down the stairs if necessary. An homunculus—the same one, or its twin—emerged from one of the doors carrying a tray with several platters on it and a decanter of wine. It walked past the cellar door without a sideways glance and disappeared around a corner to the left. Blade had drawn a stairway there—yes, she could hear the different sound to the footsteps as the homunculus mounted the stairs. The cutlery clinked faintly at every step, and Shadow counted them: twenty steps, no pauses, no hesitations. Of course, Baloran would scarcely entrap his main stairway, which he himself must use regularly. Inconveniencing the homunculus was one thing, but his own convenience was quite another.

Shadow waited until the homunculus had mounted the stairs, then carefully eased the door open. As her ears had reported earlier, this one did not squeak.

"Ready?" Shadow whispered. Blade nodded silently.

The entrance hall told Shadow a great deal about Baloran, more than Blade's stories could. The hall was lofty and impressive, but empty. The blocks of bone-white stone had been fitted as expertly as the strange shelters in the swamp, but no rug warmed the bare floor, and a single ancient tapestry—dating back nearly to the Black Wars and worth about a thousand Suns, Shadow's expert eye decided—hung on the wall. There was an elegant crystal chandelier overhead, but the candles had long since burned down to useless stubs. She had no doubt that were the castle not kept so spotlessly clean—by who or what she had no idea—the dining room would be dusty with disuse.

"What do you think?" Shadow whispered to Blade. "Go up, or wait for that thing to come back down?"

"It only took a tray up," Blade murmured back. "If it had no other duties, it would have returned by now.

Doubtless Baloran had some use for it. There is no wisdom in waiting.''

Shadow nodded and slipped cautiously along the hallway wall. She didn't like the feel of the white stone; there was something in its odd, almost oily smoothness and lack of usual stone chill that reminded her of the bone it so resembled in appearance.

The staircase up was a spiral, unlike the straight cellar stairs; Shadow realized uneasily that there would be no clear view upward—or downward, she chided herself sternly; and she would match her ears against those of any mage-born creature, no matter how ugly. Still, she felt uneasy; there was something uncanny about the place that made the small hairs on the back of her neck prickle, as if she was being watched.

Although she had no reason to suspect traps or tricks, Shadow moved as cautiously as she had up the cellar stairs—testing each step, pausing and listening before she advanced.

There was no cover at the head of the stairs, and Shadow glanced quickly about. The doors were where Blade had marked them on the sketch; that might or might not mean that the rooms were laid out as she had remembered.

"He should be in the study, most likely," Blade whispered, gesturing at the door at the end of the hall.

Shadow shook her head.

"Uh-uh."

Blade glanced at her narrowly. "Why?"

"Ten steps after it got to the top of the stairs," Shadow whispered. "Then a door click. That means either the first lab—that door on the left—or the library there on the right. Anything else is too far."

"Then we will begin with the second laboratory," Blade murmured quietly. "It is a likely enough place to start."

Shadow nodded and edged to the door on the left, which Blade had indicated was the library, and leaned close enough to the door to listen without actually pressing her ear to the door. Nothing. Either the door was too thick, or there was nothing to be heard.

She edged quietly to the first laboratory door and listened again. This time she heard a rustling sound, as if of a page being turned. Then there was a faint clink of metal—perhaps the sound of a goblet touching the edge of a metal plate.

Shadow nodded to Blade, indicating the laboratory door. Blade moved down to the door of the bedroom—if Blade's map, as it seemed, held true—and listened as Shadow had done, then tried the study door. She shook her head at each.

Shadow slipped across the hall to the second laboratory door and listened, again not touching the actual surface of the door. Nothing. She beckoned to Blade, gestured at the door, and raised her eyebrows inquiringly.

Blade touched the hilt of the black dagger, glanced back at Shadow, and, to Shadow's amazement, raised one black-gloved hand, fingers splayed, at heart level—an extremely secret gesture used by thieves of the older schools to indicate magic.

Shadow nodded, making no indication of her surprise, and reached for the extract of moly she'd brought. She pointed to the doorknob, the keyhole, the hinges, the frame, and the door itself, raising her eyebrows at Blade.

Blade touched the dagger again and glanced over the door. She pointed to the base of the door and sketched an imaginary line.

Shadow held her hand flat vertically, miming the door, and ran her finger across the bottom, raising her eyebrows.

Blade shook her head, mimed opening the door and taking a "step" with her finger, and held her palms apart about one handsbreadth.

Shadow nodded, scowling. A threshold trap—undoubtedly something to sense Baloran's identity, or his particular magical presence, so that his homunculi could enter—was a nasty, devious piece of work. But so am I, she thought, chuckling silently to herself.

She pulled on her own gloves, touched the keyhole, and whispered, ''Aufrhyr.'' She uncorked the small vial of moly and tipped the vial carefully over one glove, rubbing the extract liberally over the paper-thin leather. Pulling a strip of cloth out of her pack, she rubbed it vigorously between her anointed gloves, making sure that every inch was dampened. Then she slowly opened the door.

The laboratory might have been one of Celene's laboratories—tables and shelves laden with bottles, jars, canisters, braziers, weights, measures, and other implements. Of more interest were several boxes sitting on the tables and shelves. This room was more brightly lit—it rated ten of the glowing globes.

Shadow carefully laid the cloth over the threshold, pushing it forward until it completely covered the area Blade had indicated. She patted it smooth, pulling out the few wrinkles until it covered the entire threshold to a depth of several inches. She glanced at Blade, raising her eyebrows. Blade nodded.

Blade might trust Blackfell implicitly, but Shadow was more skeptical. Shadow motioned Blade out of the direct line of the door before she stepped in. No point in caution this time; Shadow simply jumped over the flattened cloth, holding her breath and mentally promising Fortune a hundred Suns if she could just get into this room without something foul happening to her.

Nothing happened.

Shadow motioned quickly to Blade. Blade stepped nonchalantly over the cloth, closing the door behind her but for a crack.

''Search quickly,'' Blade whispered. ''I will keep watch.''

Shadow raised her eyebrows in surprise, but shrugged. Blade was not, after all, here for the plunder.

Shadow soon had more to shake her head over than Blade's disinterest in treasure. Much of the contents of the laboratory might be of inestimable value, but Shadow had no way of knowing the worth of items and substances as esoteric as those she found. The jars and vials were neatly labeled in a very archaic form of the common tongue, one not used for several centuries in Allanmere, but that posed her no problem; she was older than the language.

To a thief accustomed to dealing in simpler merchandise, however, Baloran's laboratory yielded little but frustration. The few items she did understand—powdered gold dust, several neat gold weights, a set of platinum measuring spoons, and several small crystal cups—were frankly not worth the effort of taking away. She disgustedly pocketed the measuring spoons on the theory that coming away with nothing at all was unworthy of a Guildmistress. There was no sign of the Eye of Urex.

Blade beckoned, and Shadow took her place at the door. The hallway remained still and empty, but something still felt vaguely wrong; Shadow was glad enough to turn her senses to watching.

She jumped and nearly yelped when Blade touched her arm. Shadow turned, biting back an acid comment. Blade smiled cynically and pressed a jar into Shadow's hand.

"Rainbow dust," she whispered. "Worth at least a few thousand Suns. Now you can cease scowling. Come, we will try the library next."

Shadow grinned and put the jar into her pack. When she and Blade were over the threshold, she tweaked the cloth out of the way, pushing it into her sleeve for future use.

Unlike the laboratory, the library was neither locked nor warded. As Shadow had expected, there was little here but books; in fact, there was *room* for little but books. Books overflowed the shelves and spilled onto tables, presses, chairs, and the floor. Most were of obvious antiquity and many were in other languages. Some were in glass cases: Shadow assumed they were either important, or valuable, or both, but she made no attempt to secure any of them. It was, after all, a choice of loading her horses with books, or with treasure, and Shadow had no intention of bothering with books!

"The study," she whispered to Blade, who nodded.

The study door was more encouraging; besides being locked, Blade noted a second magical threshold trap and something on the doorknob, besides. Shadow inspected more closely and found, in addition, a tiny wire within the keyhole where her tools would surely break it. Well, no matter; she wouldn't be using her tools this time. A second vial of moly extract had to be used to treat the doorknob, but the cloth was still damp enough to allow them to cross the threshold once Shadow had opened the door with her bracelet. Nonetheless, Shadow was a little worried; she had only two more vials left.

She shook her head and slipped through the door, Blade close behind her, and closed the door before she allowed herself a quiet gasp of amazement.

Shadow would never have called this place a study, not by the broadest definition she could imagine. There was, indeed, one desk, with a book, pen and ink on it, but that desk had been pushed back against the wall as if forgotten. Flanking it were several locked glass cases and locked boxes; a rug lay pushed back, wrinkled, against their bases. Unlike the laboratory or the library, this room had windows: four of them, two on each of the outside walls, overlooking the barren heath surrounding the castle.

Obviously Baloran had some experiment in progress. Four double circles had been drawn or painted on the floor, each about a man-height across, with symbols and writings in some arcane language inscribed between the outer and inner circle of each. The circles seemed harmless enough, but Shadow made a mental note to avoid them.

Shadow stepped to the nearest case and looked inside. There were four rods inside resting on black velvet, each rod deeply incised with carvings and symbols in a surface of the same bone-white substance the castle was made of. She bent down to glance at the lock.

"Perhaps you'd simply like the key?" a voice said lightly.

Shadow turned slowly, allowing a small knife to drop inconspicuously from her sleeve into the cupped palm of her hand.

He stood in the doorway, quietly, a small smile on his face.

EIGHT ════

Shadow's first thought was, How can he be so young?

Her second thought was, What in Fortune's name is he?

He was tall, taller even than Donya, whom Shadow thought privately could touch the sky, and slender. His hair was as black as Blade's, and for a long moment she thought they might somehow be kin. Then she saw his eyes, and that illusion faded.

His eyes were black, but not as Shadow's eyes were black, or even as Blade's eyes were black. His eyes were black from top to bottom, black from side to side, the dead blackness of Spirit Lake. There was nothing to be read in those eyes; like his books, they were written in some language too arcane. His features seemed too soft for a man's, too strange.

He wore a simple black robe, light and loose, and black slippers. A simple silver circlet clasped his brow, and a bracelet in the shape of a snake with ruby eyes climbed his left wrist; but he wore no other ornamentation. His hands were long-fingered and agile, and in them he clasped an obsidian rod twined with silver.

Blade stood beside him, one hand still touching the door frame, peering out into the hall, one hand resting on the black dagger at her hip. Her eyes were wide and unblinking, and she did not move; Shadow could not even tell if she was breathing.

"Be welcome, Guildmistress Shadow," Baloran said smoothly. "I'm honored that you've chosen to visit me, albeit uninvited. But tell me, do, what are your plans for the dagger in your hand?"

"That depends," Shadow said warily, "on the nature of your hospitality."

"My hospitality?" Baloran said mildly. "You answer my hospitality with a knife. But I must thank you, after all, for returning this creature to me." He glanced over at Blade, then looked back at Shadow, smiling warmly.

"All the same, my lady thief," he continued, "I think it would be wise to take a few precautions in the name of my own safety. Therefore, I would ask that you deposit that dagger, along with all else you have, in the corner there." He nodded at the corner, then smoothly drew the dagger from Blade's belt and toyed with it, touching the tip to Blade's still throat. "I will wait here while you do so."

Shadow scowled and dropped the dagger in the corner where indicated. She took the others from her belt and deposited them also, and dropped her pack over all.

"No, no," Baloran smiled. "I've heard a great deal about you, Guildmistress. Everything, if you please, including your clothing."

Shadow grinned back, showing the second dagger she had palmed.

"I'm pretty good with this," she said, "and pretty fast, too. I might be tempted to take my chances. Besides, what makes you think I care much what happens to her?"

"I can't imagine that you do," Baloran said easily. "However, I believe there's someone here you do care for. Come in, my dear," he called out the door.

Donya stepped quietly through the door. Her armor was dirty and pitted and she herself was bruised and cut, as if she had been through battle. Her face was calm, empty.

Baloran took her hand and carefully removed her gauntlet. He touched the tip of the black dagger to her lax palm.

"I'm sure you are as quick as you say with that dagger," he said. "Then again, will you take the chance? Even if you kill me, how will you restore her?" He pressed the dagger down a bit, so it dimpled the skin of Donya's palm.

"All right!" Shadow said hurriedly, tossing her dagger into the corner. "All right."

She pulled at her clothes, hurriedly tossing each garment into the corner. She balked at the bracelet, infuriated when Baloran chuckled.

"Keep it," he said. "It will make no difference."

Naked, she turned to face him and shrugged.

"Well?" she said. "If you wanted to seduce me, there were better ways."

"Step into the circle," Baloran told her, pointing to one of the circles she had seen drawn on the ground. "That one."

Shadow stepped into the circle, sighed, and sat down.

"What now?" she asked. "Going to turn me into a swamp-croaker?"

"Not in the least. But let me be rid of this fellow; it's quite hungry now, and I'd prefer it safely bound." Baloran walked over and tossed the black dagger into a second circle; it transformed into the demon. Blackfell sat down as Shadow had done, sparing her but the briefest of glances.

"Donya, my dear," Baloran said, "will you please take Blade's belongings and place them over there, next to Shadow's. Then you may remove her clothing and place it there also."

Donya, her face blank, proceeded to obey. Blade's pack joined Shadow's on the floor, then (to Shadow's grudging amazement) an impressive collection of concealed weapons.

Shadow spared Baloran a glance; he was quite occupied with supervising Donya, who apparently required a great deal of supervision. Shadow saw Blackfell cautiously reach out a hand—

—and draw it back hurriedly at a flash of silver sparks.

Shadow bit down an exclamation of surprise, but too late; she saw Baloran watching them amusedly. He gestured with his rod; Blackfell disappeared, and the dagger rested quietly on the floor.

"As your friend can tell you," he said gently, "I'm quite an expert on bindings. Spare yourself some pain and don't test the barrier. Ah, finished, are you, my lady?"

Shadow glanced at Blade and her eyes widened. Blade's gloves and boots and her never-ending modesty suddenly made a great deal of sense. She had noticed Blade's odd skin and dark blood when they crossed the river; now she realized just how different Blade really was—as different, in her own way, as Baloran himself.

What first drew Shadow's attention, and her instinctively muffled reaction of horror and pity, were the scars. Long, deep scars ran the length of Blade's back, almost replacing the entire surface of her skin from nape to buttocks. More scars crossed Blade's shoulders and ran down the tops of her arms.

What she had seen of Blade's skin had been an odd grayish-white and uncommonly smooth, almost like scar tissue itself. Shadow now saw that the same held true over her entire body except where the white scars ran, although the grayish cast faded out near her hands, feet, and neck. Except for her black tresses, Blade was entirely hairless. But that was the least of it.

Blade's long fingers had no nails. Heavy scarring could also be seen between the fingers. Her toes ended in stumps, as if the toes had at some time been cut off short, although they were of a normal length.

"Fortune favor me," Shadow gasped involuntarily. "Did *you* do all that to her?"

Baloran turned to her, an expression of genuine surprise on his androgynous face.

"Certainly not. In fact I've never done her the slightest harm. Nor your lady here, in case you were inclined to blame her battered appearance on me—although I suppose I might indirectly bear the blame, since she did some scuffling with a few of my creations. But, of course, nobody forced her to trespass on my lands and harass my creatures, any more than anyone forced this creature to break into my home and steal my property. Ah, my dear, put her in that circle—yes, that one there," he added, gesturing to Donya. "Thank you so much."

"You don't call that harm?" Shadow growled, nodding at Donya, who was carrying Blade's immobile body to the indicated circle.

"I suppose I could have chained her in a dungeon," Baloran shrugged negligently. "This way is much more comfortable for her and less troublesome for me. But I'll free her shortly, don't worry."

Donya had placed Blade within the circle. Baloran gestured with the rod, and Blade began to stir, stiffly.

"You go in the last circle, my lady," he told Donya gently. "Armor and clothing against the wall first, however."

Donya stripped obediently and stepped into the indicated circle.

"Very good," Baloran said approvingly. "Now I can release her as well."

He gestured, and Donya jumped slightly. Immediately she sprang forward. As she reached the edge of the inner circle, silver sparks jumped at her touch, and Donya gave an involuntary cry of pain as she fell back. Where her hand had touched the magical barrier, the skin was reddened and blistering.

"Please, my lady," Baloran said, appearing pained. "As you heard me explain to your friend, I have no desire to hurt you. Be still for the present, and spare yourself some pain. There is no way to cross the barrier; it is a name-binding and, if I may be so vain, a quite tricky piece of work. Nearly as tricky, my lethal friend," he added, glancing at Blade, "as the work I did to bind the trap you stumbled into so

neatly the first time you visited. What have you to say for
my defensive measures now?''

''If anything, your powers have lessened,'' Blade snarled,
curled into as small a ball as flesh would allow. ''We
penetrated your defenses quite easily, and it was not they
that captured us in the end, but you yourself.''

Baloran chuckled delightedly.

''Why, then I have surpassed myself!'' he laughed.
''Indeed, I was at some trouble to determine how to get you
into my castle without killing you both, and yet convince
you that you had indeed managed to bypass my defenses
successfully.''

''You couldn't have known we were coming,'' Shadow
accused him. ''Donya herself didn't know, and Blade said
we were protected from any magical detection.''

''And you are correct,'' Baloran told her. ''But I'm very
disappointed in you, mistress thief, if you believe my only
resources are magical. Why, I've been to Allanmere several
times since you've left, and your disappearance is all the
gossip of the town. Given that it corresponded so neatly to
the theft of the Eye of Urex, and given Donya's kind
information that you yourself had provided her with the
history of the gem and that she had left you a map to the
area of my home, it took only the simplest of calculations to
deduce where you had gone.''

''It should've been even easier than that,'' Shadow said
with a shrug. ''When you took the gem and made it look
like I'd done it, you should've known I'd have almost no
choice but to find it, or let the Council of Churches squash
the Guild like a pesky gnat. Your plan must've allowed for
me showing up on your doorstep.''

''Hardly.'' Baloran smiled gently. ''I am terribly sorry to
malign the excellent research you've done to find me and
link me to the Eye of Urex, but unfortunately I have to tell
you that your conclusion was entirely wrong.''

''Wrong.'' Shadow laughed. ''Your words have the odor

of a cow pasture. I suppose you mean to tell me that the Eye of Urex was never yours, eh?''

"On the contrary; it was one of my more valuable possessions at one time," Baloran shrugged. "I was quite disturbed when it disappeared. But it had, after all, served its purpose. I was rather more disturbed that someone had stolen it than that it had been stolen, if you understand me. Therefore I attended to the former rather than the latter, you see, and moved to protect myself.

"I've known for some time that the Temple of Urex had my orb," he shrugged. "One can scarcely conceal a mage's own magic from him. But what did that matter? I no longer needed it. Surely your researches, Guildmistress, have shown how long the Temple of Urex has had it. Why would I steal it now?"

"That's what I'd like to know," Shadow said. "What's more, I'd like to know why you took it at such a time and in such a way that everyone thinks I'd done it."

Baloran laughed.

"So would I, Guildmistress, so would I. The plain fact is that I did not. I did not plan to use you as a scapegoat for the theft, and in fact, I did not commit the theft. I am sorry to disappoint you, Guildmistress, after your clever research and your arduous journey, but this time you have the wrong culprit."

"So you said," Donya said sourly. "Or the thing that claimed to be you. But why should we believe that?"

Baloran shrugged. "Because it is the truth. It scarcely matters, however," he said gently, "the situation being as it is. What matters is the number of problems you have caused me—the three of you here, my lady's guardsmen who are arriving to storm my gates even as we speak, and the gods alone know how many people now know of my hitherto well-concealed home. It really is quite annoying." He sighed.

"Well, I'm sure your annoyance is going to hurt us worse than you," Shadow said grimly.

"Quite the contrary." Baloran crossed to a decanter of wine, poured himself a glass. "Why should I do you any harm? Lady Donya approached me quite properly; she was quite prepared to talk politely before her guardsmen stormed my castle with lances and swords at the ready. If she fails to return to Allanmere hale and healthy, no doubt I would face all the military might that the High Lord and Lady could muster, no matter how far or how often I moved my keep.

"You, my fair Guildmistress, have done little more than rather cleverly make your way into my castle and inspect a few of my goods. Yes, you've necessitated that I move my castle once more, but if I killed you, I'd only rouse the anger of your many supporters in Allanmere, and that would make any further dealings in town very uncomfortable. Besides, Guildmistress, you've done me the favor of bringing me a gift I appreciate greatly." He glanced at Blade and the dagger. "I have never felt quite safe with that venomous beast running loose with the dagger, which she'd no doubt die happily to plunge into my flesh."

He sipped his wine thoughtfully.

"No, I have no reason to harm either of you, and several very good reasons to let you leave unharmed. Therefore you will both be freed on Lady Donya's word that you will both leave quietly, taking her troops with you, and trouble me no further. Given the depth of your friendship with her, Guildmistress, which she quite involuntarily divulged to me, I am sure you will honor her oath, knowing that if she breaks it I am quite capable—magically and mentally—of finding her and rendering her life even more short than is usual for humans."

Shadow laughed shortly. "So you think that in exchange for your dubious assurance of our safety—so long as we do what you want, that is—I'll walk quietly away without the Eye of Urex which I've repeatedly almost gotten myself killed for, and also leaving Blade to your mercy? Is that your idea of a bargain?"

Baloran smiled apologetically. "It is, unfortunately, the best I'm prepared to offer. The Eye of Urex, as you so charmingly insist on calling it, I cannot give to you as I do not have it. If you like, however, I'll address a missive to Lord Vikram stating falsely that I took it and stating my claim upon the gem, which can, as you've already discovered, be historically verified. The Council of Churches is no threat to *me*.

"As to Blade," he continued, "you must admit that my claim is just. She has robbed me and attempted my life—surely you will not deny that is her purpose here—and I am entitled to deal with her as I see fit, she not being within the demesnes of Allanmere's law.

"Besides," he said, looking craftily at Donya, "I doubt many in Allanmere would protest her disappearance. There might be many who would thank me for relieving the city of so lethal an assassin."

Shadow glanced at Blade, who still said nothing, her eyes locked on Baloran. Given the expression on Blade's face, Shadow had to admit that she was a lethal-looking person, even sitting naked on the floor.

"What do you say, Lady of Allanmere and Heir to the throne?" Baloran said lightly to Donya. "What do you think of my bargain, and how would you advise your friend?"

Donya's lips tightened whitely with anger, but she looked at Shadow and slowly nodded.

"Shady . . . I don't like it any better than you do," Donya said slowly. "But I don't see that we've got any choice. Let the Council of Churches take their quarrel to him, if they're that eager. Take the letter and the problem's solved; that's what we both came for, isn't it?"

"You can't mean," Shadow said, staring at her friend, "that you want me to just leave her here with him."

"No, I don't," Donya exclaimed. "But I can't do anything to stop him from whatever he wants to do with her. What do you want *me* to do? Shady, I don't understand you.

She's an assassin, and if she's who I think she is, she's the same one who tried to kill you last year! I don't know what kind of deal you worked up with her—I don't want to know, either—but she's not worth both our lives and the lives of all my guard and the downfall of the Guild, which will happen when you don't come back. Besides, you know what the penalty is for assassination. Baloran can't possibly do any worse to her than the law would in Allanmere.''

"I'm not so sure of that," Shadow began, but Donya interrupted.

"And I suppose you expected me to keep quiet about her, too," Donya said hotly. "Shadow, do you have any idea what would happen if the Heir was found to be helping an assassin avoid arrest? Not to mention the most infamous assassin in Allanmere?"

"I didn't expect you to ever know about it," Shadow sighed exasperatedly. "I planned to be in and out of here quickly before you even got here. I did it to keep your overly scrupulous ass from getting killed by this same pox-rotted mage you'd like to leave Blade to!"

"Well, that's hardly my responsibility," Donya protested. "I did my best to keep you from coming here at all. I'm not responsible for Blade and whatever grudge she and Baloran have between them. I *am* responsible for what happens between the Guild and the Council of Churches over this mess, and so are you, and I don't understand why you're ready to throw that responsibility to the current over her!"

"You did it for me," Shadow said pointedly.

"That's different," Donya cried. "Damn all, Shady, you've saved my life!"

"Yes," Shadow nodded. "And she's saved mine."

Shadow glanced at Blade. This time Blade's eyes were on her, and in them Shadow saw an expression she could not read. Contempt, most likely.

"How interesting," Baloran said, strolling over. He took a ring of keys from his pocket and unlocked the case

Shadow had seen, extracting one of the rods from the velvet.
He pulled a chair out from the wall and sat down. "Do you
know, I'd have said before this that the alliance of an
ordinary elvan thief with the Heir to the throne of Allanmere
was the most unlikely I'd heard of. But you do continue to
surprise me, Shadow. I enjoy that, so in return I'll do you
something of a favor and show you just what you've chosen
to ally yourself with."

He began chanting, the wand pointed at Blade. Slowly, a
mist began to form just outside the circle. It swirled, dark
oily smoke twisting like a thing alive. Slowly it began to
compact, writhing into a form that became more recogniz-
able.

It was Blade—and it was not.

It was generally Blade's height, and Shadow recognized
the lithe build and that grayish, preternaturally smooth skin.
There was something familiar in the set of the large, slightly
slanting eyes, although they were amber-gold instead of
black, as was the long, trailing hair. The mouth was too
wide, however, and the brow too sloping—the ears and nose
oddly small on the wide head—and the neck was ridged
with odd folds of skin that Shadow thought might be gills.
The long-fingered hands were Blade's own, but thin mem-
branes of tough skin stretched between each digit. The toes
were also long and spread widely, and similarly webbed.

Blade—the Blade Shadow knew in the circle—let out a
howl, a horrible inhuman sound Shadow had heard only
once before, on a night beside Spirit Lake in the swamp. She
had thought then that nothing human could have made that
sound; now she knew that she had been right.

Blade howled again, a bone-chilling cry of despair the
like of which Shadow could only guess at, and hurled
herself at the image. Silver sparks flew again, and again, as
Blade threw herself against the magical barrier. The barrier
sizzled and spat, and Shadow could smell the growing scent
of burning flesh fill the room, but Blade threw herself
against the barrier relentlessly, howling and flailing with her

hands, until Baloran gestured and the image dissolved. He spoke a sharp word and gestured again, and Blade collapsed limply to the floor, sobbing quietly without tears.

"Odd little thing, isn't she?" Baloran said idly, gazing at her. "That's not precisely how she looked when she came here before, but magic knows its business. Phew, what an odor. Burnt eel, it smells like."

He chuckled a little at his own humor.

"So you think transforming her was such a punishment," Donya said icily. "Frankly I find it rather an improvement."

Blade moaned, and Baloran chuckled again.

"Wrong again, my lady," he said. "Why, the thing was in and out of my castle before I knew it, despite my best efforts to protect my goods. As eager as you may be to lay the blame at my feet, I no more transformed her than I am responsible for those scars you winced at. How she came by them I have no idea, but the alteration in her appearance I can guess at.

"Long exposure to demonic magic alters living things," Baloran shrugged. "I myself have changed much over the years, and the animals in the area—as doubtless you have noticed—have changed also. A demon is very powerful magic, you know; that's one reason I rarely keep one around long. Not to mention their varied and nasty feeding habits."

"You mean the demon changed her like that?" Shadow asked curiously.

"Of course," Baloran shrugged. "My trap was set to bind the two together, bind their souls. Its very demonic magic feeds her and prolongs her life. She has absorbed a great deal of its demonic nature, wouldn't you say?"

Donya looked inclined to agree, but to Baloran's obvious surprise, Shadow threw back her head and laughed heartily.

"Oh, my," she gasped. "Baloran, you've been living out here on the fringes too long. What were you wanting me to do? Scream and cover my eyes? Beg you to kill her and rid the world of her? I'm Guildmistress of the Guild of Thieves,

Fortune favor me, not a highborn lady. I wanted Blade to help me, not bed me. Come to think of it, I've bedded men who looked worse.''

"Ah, but were you willing to give your life for them?" Baloran asked gently. "Think carefully. My bargain is generous but I won't repeat it too many more times."

"You don't need to repeat it," Donya said quietly. "If Blade saved Shady's life, that's enough for me, whatever she is. Or was."

"Blade!" Baloran laughed. "Even her name is a lie. Her name is Amber, if you would believe it. Taking a name to hide her own! That's a new trick, and quite clever, too, I'll admit. I learned it, however, from a few of her earliest acquaintances in Allanmere, against just such an occasion as this, when I might want to cast a name-binding."

Shadow raised an eyebrow. "Well, I don't care what her name is," she said. "She's my—yes—my friend, I suppose, and you'll wait a long time and exhaust a lot of breath before you'll convince me to walk away and leave her here to you."

Baloran shrugged sadly. "Then I suppose I must leave her to you," he said. "What a pity."

"How do you mean that?" Donya asked warily.

Baloran gestured at the dagger. "Why do you think I've kept it in that form? In its own form it's bound to harm no ensouled creature, but it can act independently to some extent—so long as it obeys the one it's bound to. As a dagger it cannot act itself, but it can kill and feed if wielded by another. Under her control, you say. But that ends when it grows too hungry, for she belongs to it as surely as it belongs to her. And now it's hungry. Very hungry, I think. Likely it's been quite active on the journey here.

"No, it would be dangerous for me to kill the Guildmistress of the Thieves' Guild of Allanmere, and the Heir as well," he continued. "But I'm sure Allanmere has come to know well the style of Blade's work. I can then return the bodies to Allanmere and swear under truthspell, if neces-

sary, that I never harmed either of you, and that I killed the
assassin myself.''

He gestured, and Blade fell out of her circle, sprawling
limply on the stone floor. Her skin was burned, severely in
places, but she crawled determinedly across the floor toward
her pack and her clothes.

Baloran watched dispassionately as Blade pulled the
clothes over her burned skin.

"You appear to be lacking something," he said amusedly. ''What could it be? Ah, your favorite weapon!''

He gestured, and the dagger rose from its circle and flew
to Blade's hand. Blade clutched it tightly, so tightly that the
burns over her knuckles split and bled.

"All this trouble," Shadow sighed, ''and I still don't
understand. You could have had me killed, or killed me
yourself, anytime if that's what you wanted. You could've
even had someone pay Blade to do it if that was what you
wanted. She damned near got me the first time somebody
did that—she would've, too, with time. I still don't understand all this trouble now, when all you'll get out of it is the
gem and our dead bodies, and having to move your castle on
top of it all!''

Baloran shook his head regretfully. ''You'll die disbe-
lieving me," he said kindly, ''but I will not have the gem,
for I do not have it now. And the dead bodies are your
decision, not mine.''

"Why should we believe someone who's killing us?''
Donya said sarcastically. ''Pardon me, having us killed.''

"Because he tells the truth." Blade's voice was ragged
with pain or perhaps from her screaming, but it was loud
enough to draw their gaze. She reached into her pack and
pulled out the Eye of Urex. ''He does not have it, because
he never took it.''

Donya gasped in amazement; even Shadow's jaw dropped.
Baloran, however, exploded into delighted laughter.

"Oh, my," he gasped. ''This is truly delightful. My dear,
odd little creature, you've actually managed to surprise me,

and how I love being surprised! And what do you plan to do with it?''

''I plan to offer you a bargain,'' Blade gritted out, moving closer. She held out the gem in one hand, the dagger in the other. ''You seem to like bargains, and I think this one will please you. Free me of this curse you have set upon me and the gem is yours once more.''

''But as I have told you, I no longer need it,'' Baloran smiled as she approached. ''You must offer me more than that. What if I demand of you what I asked of your— friends? If I free you, will you leave peaceably, leaving them behind for me? I might agree to that; after all, if I free you, you will be only one more ordinary person, and after I move my home, you would likely never be able to find me again.''

Blade glanced at Shadow and Donya, her face impassive. ''Yes,'' she said. ''I will agree to that.''

Baloran chuckled. ''And if I bid you kill them first?''

''Yes.''

Donya gave a little snort of disgust. ''Shady, you are the single *worst* judge of human nature I've ever seen,'' she groaned. ''If she represents your taste in friends, I'm *insulted.*''

Shadow shrugged. ''Sorry,'' she said abashedly.

''Delightful,'' Baloran laughed. ''What an amoral beast I've created! But you see, my dear, I've no quarrel with them at all, which is not the case with you. So tell me, then, what you'll do if I decline your bargain.''

''Then I will give you something else,'' Blade said from between clenched teeth. She extended the dagger. ''I will give you this. Blackfell will be glad enough to taste your blood.''

''What a terrible choice,'' Baloran sighed. He drummed his fingers on the chair arm. ''No, though it pains me, I'm afraid I must refuse.''

Blade screamed again, this time a very human scream of raw fury, and dashed the Eye of Urex to the ground, where it exploded into a thousand glowing fragments. She leaped forward, thrusting the dagger at Baloran's heart—

—only to suddenly abort her leap, twisting aside to slam to the stone of the floor.

Baloran looked at her sympathetically.

"That must have hurt," he said. "But you may try again, if you like."

Panting, Blade dragged herself up from the floor, blind fury in her eyes, and again thrust with the dagger.

The tip stopped a bare inch from Baloran's heart and hung there, quivering. Every muscle in Blade's arm trembled, but slowly she drew the dagger back. She collapsed to the floor, her breath rasping, and stared at Baloran disbelievingly.

"There may be," he said gently, "two other mages in the world more skilled than I at bindings, but there are not three. Did you think that my binding affected Blackfell alone? No. You I bound, secretly, that you could do me no harm. Otherwise I should never have freed you, you see; otherwise I would have spent these years finding you and destroying you, lest you come to turn my soul-eating demon against me. Indeed, I've kept an intermittent watch on you in Allanmere, especially lately when you seemed to become more active, more visible, in the unlikely event that you had found someone capable of breaking the binding. But I knew I really had nothing to fear. So you could never have forced me to free you."

"But what about the gem?" Shadow asked, looking unhappily at the gleaming shards. "You didn't even want it!"

"No." Baloran chuckled. "I did not. But I will tell you an interesting story. You see, magic is a fleeting thing. It must be sustained somehow, or it is quickly gone. Your circles, you see, are sustained by you—by the power of your names. Other spells I've sustained by giving them a permanent housing—these rods, for example. A potion is another way of sustaining magic, or delaying it.

"Summoning a demon, you see," he continued, "is a most strenuous exercise. Controlling them and keeping them on our plane is even more difficult. So how to bring a demon, keep him and bind him indefinitely? Simple. I confined that magic to a solid and lasting article. A gem."

He toed one of the bright shards.

"So you see, my dear," he said to Blade, "I no longer had a use for that gem unless I had wanted to do as you asked and reverse the spell, which I had no interest in doing. That was, of course, its only value."

Blade made a small sound, perhaps a whimper. One hand reached out to touch one of the small shards, from which the glow was already fading. The dagger dropped from her hand.

"And now," Baloran said briskly, "I will leave the three of you together. I have my lady's guard to deal with now—I can see them in my yard—and it will be quite amusing to wager to myself which of you she will kill. Eventually, of course, it will be both, but the survivor will have another chance to bargain with me, perhaps."

"Baloran!" Shadow called, waiting until he turned. She deliberately took the combs from her hair, letting the black braids fall seductively to trail on the floor.

"With three naked women at your disposal, surely you can think of something better to do than kill them," she purred.

Baloran looked at her and chuckled.

"The extensive practice of strong magic tends to damp the baser urges," he said regretfully. "However, should Blade choose to kill your friend and spare you, perhaps we can discuss the subject at another time." He turned back toward the door.

"I doubt it," Shadow said grimly. She slid the tiny blades from their concealed sheaths in her hair combs and threw them.

Only a movement of almost preternatural swiftness saved Baloran's life; he half turned, perhaps alerted by the tone of

Shadow's voice, and raised one arm protectively. One of the tiny blades sliced into his raised forearm; the other embedded itself solidly near his elbow. Both cuts oozed blood that was so dark as to be nearly black.

Baloran slowly lowered his arm, his expression incredulous rather than angry. He inspected his arm, gingerly plucking the embedded blades loose, a smile slowly spreading over his face.

"Excellent!" he said, his grin widening. "Truly remarkable. My lady Guildmistress, you are quite a resourceful adversary. What delightful games we could have played, under other circumstances."

"I may have a stone or two to drop yet," Shadow said coldly, stifling her disappointment.

"I'm sure you have," Baloran smiled back. "I'll be interested to see how the stakes change."

Then he was gone. Shadow heard the lock click behind him.

As soon as the door shut, Shadow briskly picked up the discarded combs and pinned her hair back up.

"Blade!" she called. "Can you get either of us out of these things?"

"No." Blade sat where she was, on the floor, gazing fixedly at the broken gem.

"What about the door? The windows?" Shadow pressed. "Come on, Blade. Do you want your revenge, or don't you?"

Blade slowly, painfully pushed herself to her feet as if all the strength had washed out of her. Leaving the dagger where she had dropped it, she walked to the door and reached for the knob. Her hand stopped before it touched; Shadow could see her skin flatten against an invisible barrier.

"Warded," Blade said stonily. She moved to the nearest window, then turned back. "The same."

"What's going on outside?" Donya called. "Can you see the guards? What's happening?"

"They are stationed mostly on the far side of the ditch," Blade said listlessly. "A few have crossed over with what appears to be a tree cut to a battering ram, but they have abandoned it. They have built a fire against the doors. The wood is charring somewhat."

"What about the barrier?" Shadow asked. "What about all those skeletons we saw? Hasn't anything happened to the guards?"

Blade shook her head. "No."

"He knows they wouldn't leave without me," Donya said. "Likely he dropped the barrier so he could send something out. Is there anything else out there that you can see?"

"No." Blade turned from the door, walked back, and picked up the dagger. She turned it in her hands thoughtfully.

"How about our clothes and gear?" Shadow suggested. "I wouldn't mind being dressed while we talk."

Blade said nothing, but she walked slowly, wearily over to where the gear was piled. She picked up Shadow's clothes and Donya's, then tossed the clothing to them. It passed easily through the circles. Shadow dressed hurriedly.

"How about our weapons now?" Shadow suggested. "And the rest of my gear. The moly may get us out of these circles."

Blade was silent a long moment. "No," she said at last.

"You can't mean that," Shadow said. "Look, when Donya and I are free, I can open that door with the bracelet. We can find Baloran and kill him. We'll figure something out."

"No." Blade looked down at the dagger again. "He is mine. He will keep me for a time, perhaps to serve him, perhaps only to amuse him, but he will keep me—for a time. I must wait, be patient until I find a way to break through the binding he set on me. And to be patient, Blackfell must feed."

"Well, then, we'll find one of his damned servants—homunculi, you called them," Shadow said crossly.

"They have no souls," Blade said. "They are only flesh animated by Baloran's magic."

"Well, Fortune favor me, you can't just walk over here and kill one of us," Shadow said exasperatedly. "With the three of us, we can escape."

"I am sorry." Blade's voice was dead as the blackness within Baloran's eyes. "But I have waited too long, I have searched too far, I have given too much. Escape is not enough. I might never have this chance again. It took me decades to plan this, decades before you came."

Shadow squatted, watching Blade carefully. "What do you mean?" she said.

"I could not locate Baloran myself," Blade said. She glanced up. "I had no connections, no one willing to sell me information. I barely managed to learn of the connection of the Eye of Urex with Baloran. I hoped it was something he might want, something he might bargain for. So I waited, waited down the long years, waited for someone to come who had the resources to locate him. And you came, finally."

"And you nearly killed me," Shadow protested.

"I did not expect someone in the Guild of Thieves to be my key," Blade confessed. "And it took some time for you to gain the standing and the contacts to be able to find the information needed. There remained only to motivate you to do so."

"So you stole the Eye of Urex," Shadow nodded. "The Council of Churches would, of course, blame me, forcing me to try to learn who'd really done it."

Blade nodded. "Perhaps you will believe that I did not mean for you to be personally involved," she said. "I expected you to hire spies, perhaps, to investigate. You surprised me by discovering the connection between Baloran and myself, by finding a way actually to me. It surpassed all my expectations. I had only to follow you to

Baloran, and you were prepared even to aid me in my purpose.''

"Well, it was a pretty convincing trick," Shadow admitted. "You played me like an expert, and Fortune favor me, I was ready to believe every word you said. It all made sense.''

"I had centuries to plan every word," Blade agreed. "If I had planned better, you would not be here. Neither you nor her." She nodded at Donya.

"Well, we are here," Donya snapped. "And largely by your doing, it seems. You owe us something better than death.''

"I owe you nothing," Blade said coldly. "If I could have prevented your coming, I would have done so. If I speak of debts . . .''

She turned and glanced at Shadow. "There is something of a debt between us," she said slowly. "Therefore Blackfell will not drink your life if I can find a way to spare you.''

"Oh, thank you," Shadow said expansively. "So you'll simply kill my best friend instead? Can't you at least let her out of that circle and give her a weapon so she'll have a chance? If you'll do that I'll give you the bracelet, tell you how to use it. Then you can get out of the room.''

Blade shook her head. "That would be an honorable thing to do," she said, "but I have no place for honor in my life. I cannot take the chance that she might kill me. You know what would happen then. And the bracelet would avail me nothing, for in the room or out of it I cannot strike at Baloran now. I must wait and find an opportunity, as long as he lets me live.''

"Well, we both stayed on your account," Shadow said. "We could have walked away and left you to whatever fate Baloran has in mind for you. Doesn't that count for something?''

"It means you were fools," Blade shrugged. "I have gained nothing by your foolishness, and you have lost much. You should have gone. In your place I would have. Anyone with any wits would have.''

''That's what I told you,'' Donya growled. ''Do me a favor and don't introduce me to any more of your friends, please? Oh, never mind, you won't have a chance to.''

''Stop it, Doe,'' Shadow said, never taking her eyes from Blade's. ''You're not helping.''

Donya threw up her hands. ''Help who?'' she demanded. ''It sounds to me as if I'm the one needing help! Who am I supposed to be helping? Her?''

''Maybe.'' Shadow sat back down inside her circle. ''Listen, Blade, or Amber, or whatever, look out the window again, will you please?''

Blade looked. ''Nothing at this moment. The fire has charred the door a little more.''

''Then there's a little time,'' Shadow said. ''When the guard attacks, Baloran will have his attention on them, on dealing with them. He won't be paying attention to us. He thinks we're safely imprisoned here. I can get us out of this room and then we can strike when he's not expecting us.''

Again Blade was silent for a moment. Then she shook her head.

''I cannot do as you say,'' she said.

''Listen to Shadow,'' Donya urged. ''This may be the only chance you'll have to see Baloran dead. Kill us and you're doing exactly what he wants. We'll be dead and you'll be in his power—and of the three of us, you're the only one he knows can't harm him. You can't expect him to release you from the binding spell.''

Blade looked down at the dagger in her hand. Her hand was clenched whitely around the black hilt, and her entire hand and arm were trembling.

''I cannot do as you say,'' she repeated.

Shadow suddenly remembered the night at Spirit Lake when Blade's hands had clenched trembling around the dagger like that, the dagger poised to pierce her own flesh, and she suddenly understood what Baloran had meant about the dagger and its hunger. The simple fact was that Blade no longer had a voice in the matter.

Shadow glanced over at her belongings at the wall, not more than a man-height away. There was no way she could persuade Blade to bring her a weapon, but—

"Well, listen," Shadow said quickly. "As you say, there are certain debts between you and me, so I think I'm entitled to ask you two favors."

"Ask," Blade said expressionlessly. "Ask quickly."

"Give me my bottle of Dragon's Blood," Shadow said. "If I have to watch my best friend killed, I'd just as soon be good and drunk."

"Shadow!" Donya protested.

"Very well," Blade said after a moment. She pulled the bottle from Shadow's pack and rolled it through the circles to her. "What else do you wish of me?"

Shadow pulled the crystal stopper from the flask and took a good-sized gulp, feeling the potent liquor burning its way to her stomach. She shuddered violently.

"She *is* my best friend," Shadow said hoarsely. "I don't want her to suffer. Go over there and make it quick, that's all I ask."

"Damn all, Shadow!" Donya shouted. "What do you think you're doing?"

"That's all I ask," Shadow repeated, looking into Blade's eyes.

"Very well," Blade said at last. "I am not merciful by nature, but I can grant you that request."

"Oh, thank you, Shadow," Donya said sarcastically. "Wouldn't want her to miss, would you?"

Shadow looked away from the expression of betrayal in her friend's eyes.

"If it's a choice of dying quickly or dying slowly, no, I wouldn't," she said. She took a second swallow from the bottle and stoppered it. "Go on, get it over with, will you?"

Blade nodded, giving Shadow a look that Shadow preferred to interpret as sympathy, and turned toward Donya's circle. Time seemed to slow, almost to stop, as Shadow saw Donya crouch, ready to defend herself as best she could, and Blade raised the black dagger—

—and Shadow leaped, forearms guarding her face.

Fire danced over her skin as silver sparks sizzled against her, but she ignored it; she bit her tongue, drawing blood as she crashed into Blade's back, but she ignored that, too. Even as she knocked Blade to the floor, she was swinging the crystal flask to crack sharply against the back of Blade's skull.

Blade made some sound—a small cry, perhaps—and was still.

"Shadow!" Donya was crouching as close to the inner edge of the circle as she could without touching it. "Are you all right?"

"I think so." Shadow looked down at herself, hissing as she touched burned flesh, but had to chuckle slightly as her charred clothes flaked away. "I think it mostly got me where I wasn't covered. You?"

"I'm fine." Donya shook her head exasperatedly. "A pox on you, Shady, and these damned games you play! You really had me believing you!"

"Well, what's important is that I had Blade believing me," Shadow grinned. "But wait a minute. I've got to get her tied up and gagged." She rummaged rope from her pack.

"She's not dead?"

Shadow laid a hand over Blade's heart, then felt the back of her head.

"No, no thanks to me. I didn't mean to hit her so hard, but I was so scared that if I hadn't ashed my pants I'd have soiled them."

"Shadow—" Donya began.

"Uh-uh," Shadow shook her head. "Don't even *think* about it. I'm going to tie her good and gag her—she's not going to thank me for these ropes on her burns—and I'm going to take the dagger with me. Then we're going to take care of Baloran and get out of here. After that, what she does is her business.''

''Shadow,'' Donya said exasperatedly. ''*How* did you get out of that binding?''

Shadow grinned as she knotted the rope.

''He was surprised that Blade had taken a new name,'' she said. ''He knew of me by reputation—that means from people in Allanmere. That means he used the name 'Shadow' in the name-binding, and that's not my true name, so I could pass through it. I gambled that you hadn't told him that Nightshade was my real name, because he liked to gloat; I figured he'd have wanted to show off that knowledge, too.''

''But it burned you,'' Donya protested.

''I expected it,'' she said. ''You can't use a nickname for decades without it becoming somewhat your own name. But it's not enough to hold me. There. Let's hope these knots are enough to hold *her*.''

The cloth soaked in moly extract was almost dry; Shadow was unsure whether it would work dry, so she used the remaining vial of moly. There would be little more occasion to use it.

Shadow laid the cloth over both the outer and inner circles of Donya's prison, covering the characters between the circles also.

''Test it first,'' Shadow warned her. ''I'm not familiar with this kind of magic.''

Donya gingerly extended a finger past the inner circle, then a hand. There was no reaction. Donya, built much larger and sturdier than Shadow, had to turn sideways to pass over the narrow cloth with safety.

The first thing she did was to sweep Shadow into a hug so vigorous that it had several effects: Shadow's feet were lifted well off the ground, the rest of her clothing crumbled away, and the breath was squeezed out of her lungs.

''I don't know whether to thank you or beat you bloody,'' Donya scowled. ''What a fright you gave me!''

"Well, thank me," Shadow gasped. "I'm in enough pain now."

"Mmmh." Donya put her down and briskly began putting on her clothes. She tossed Shadow her inner shirt.

"Put that on," she said. "It'll hide your burns and make Baloran wonder why his trick didn't work."

Shadow belted the shirt at her waist—it hung nearly to her knees—and rolled the sleeves up halfway, tying them at her wrists with cord. She hung two daggers at her belt, then took the sheath from another, into which she securely wedged the black dagger.

"Shady, look!" Donya called from the window, her voice catching slightly.

Shadow scurried over as quickly as she could, shirttails flapping around her buttocks.

"What is it?"

"Look."

Donya's guardsmen were no longer waiting outside the door; nor were they any longer alone. Now they were fighting for their lives.

Several guards lay dead on the lawn, but Shadow suspected it was not the sight of the dead guards that had caused Donya's gasp; she was a seasoned warrior, and she and Shadow had together seen—indeed, done—much worse. No, it was not the dead guardsmen that horrified Donya.

It was what had killed them—what was killing them.

They were soldiers, strictly speaking, in the same sense that Blade was a human. Perhaps they had once *been* human. Their armor, however, was dulled by rust and old blood, caked with dirt, and pierced by ancient weapons, some of which remained in the wounds. Tatters of cloth or leather and flesh hung from partially exposed bones. Noxious black fluid dripped from rotting eyes, noses, and mouths and anywhere the guards' weapons struck them, but the revenants appeared undaunted by their wounds. As Shadow watched, the captain sheared off his gruesome opponent's arm. It dropped to the ground, only to crawl forward by the fingers; its previous owner appeared uncaring of the loss, fighting on with its single arm.

"How fast can you open the door?" Donya asked, turning and drawing her sword. It was a little longer than Shadow.

"Watch this." Shadow reached out until she touched the invisible barrier in front of the door.

"Aufrhyr."

Her hand continued forward until she touched the doorknob and the lock.

"Aufrhyr."

The door opened.

"So what's the plan?" Shadow asked.

Donya said nothing; her lips were set thinly and lightning flashed in her eyes as she stormed through the door, naked sword first.

"Oh, *that* plan," Shadow shrugged. "You know, Doe," she began as she followed, "I imagine Baloran's got the door—"

Crash!

"—locked," Shadow finished. "Never mind, I guess it's not."

She turned back to glance at Blade, who was beginning to stir feebly in her bonds. From somewhere behind her came Donya's voice, raised in rage, and the clash of metal against metal. Shadow hesitated.

She drew a dagger from her belt, glanced at the bright steel blade, then slid it across the floor so that it lay at Blade's feet.

She turned and followed the sound of Donya's voice.

The door to Baloran's other laboratory was not only open; it was hanging askew on its hinges, and the frame nearest the doorknob was splintered and broken. Shadow had to chuckle at that, but her moment of amusement was brief.

The laboratory looked much like the other one but that

there were only a few potions, powders, and herbs, most of
which were now spilled on the floor. A large wooden table,
together with the books and parchment that had once rested
on it, was now lying on the floor also.

Most of the floor had—previously—been cleared. There
were two concentric circles marked on the floor with arcane
symbols between them; however, unlike the chalked circles
in the laboratory, this one was permanently incised into the
stone. A pentagram was inside the circle, and Baloran was
seated on a platform inside the pentagram. From where he
sat, he could see comfortably out the window.

At the moment, however, his attention appeared divided
between the combat going on in his yard and that taking
place in his study.

Donya had wisely chosen a position in one corner where
two cabinets guarded her back. At the front, however, were
two of the revenants. Three swords—two rusted and chipped,
one shining bright—flashed so rapidly that Shadow could
barely see her friend. Another revenant hovered behind the
two, looking for an opening, and Shadow could hear more
feet mounting the stairs.

As Shadow took this in, the third revenant near Donya
turned to face her, at least to the extent that it did, in fact,
have a face. Shadow yelped and dodged behind a fallen
table; the revenant had a sword almost as long as Donya's
and three times her reach at least. As she dodged, the two
daggers flew from her hands.

The daggers thunked home, drawing some black, bilious
fluid from the revenant's rotting body, but the revenant
seemed to mind not at all, any more than the ones in the yard
had. It came after her slowly but steadily; she was much
quicker and could probably manage to stay out of its reach
as long as she had somewhere to run, but nothing was going
to hinder it.

She reluctantly drew the black dagger from its sheath. It
was colder now than it had been before, and the cold seemed
to seize her hand. She could feel its hunger, its desire to

taste blood and pain and death. She shuddered, but dared not put it back. It was all she had left. She doubted it would have any effect on the revenants, but—

Perhaps she could lure the revenant away from the room long enough that Donya might defeat her two, or perhaps it would cease fighting when it left Baloran's area of attention. Shadow glanced at the door.

Too late. Three more corpses were already pushing clumsily in through the doorway. These were also armored; Shadow realized irrelevantly that these were likely barbarian soldiers from the Black Wars.

Her moment of inattention nearly cost her her arm as a rusty sword swept down to embed itself in the tabletop beside her; only near-perfect reflexes saved her, and she gained a precious moment to escape while the revenant pried its blade loose from the polished wood.

But now there was a new problem. One of the newly entered revenants had moved to join the two near Donya; the other two were coming for her. In the small, cluttered room, she could not hope to dodge three of them for long. They were careful, however, she noted, to keep themselves between her and Baloran. That was something to consider.

If, of course, they gave her time to consider anything at all. She doubted they would.

Shadow glanced around frantically. She saw a chair, grabbed it, and threw it in the path of the approaching revenant. Her quickness paid off. The revenant stumbled and fell, crashing resoundingly against the stones, and its sword shattered; she gained a little time as it painstakingly climbed back to its feet. But now the second one had moved to flank her and the third was closing in from the other side.

She inhaled a whiff of a horrible boneyard stench as a rotting hand grasped her arm. Shadow pulled away furiously, but it was too strong. A second arm was reaching for her throat—

Suddenly the arm holding her fell away, landing on the floor beside the arm reaching for her. The skeletal hand still clutched at her arm, but Shadow danced away, shaking vigorously at her arm until the hand fell.

One of the revenants' heads followed the severed limbs and now Shadow could see what had happened; Blade stood there, a short sword in her hands and a look of cold fury in her eyes, for the moment thankfully too busy to see where the dagger had gone. Shadow grinned and fled, leaving the revenants to one far more qualified than she to deal with them.

Perhaps she could now manage to get closer to Baloran. But the room was crowded now, and there were more revenants in the doorway. How many, she couldn't be sure through the twisting and moving bodies.

Shadow used a single upright chair as a springboard to leap onto the top of a low bookshelf. She ran along it, then abandoned her road when the shelf started to topple. She jumped to a tabletop, lithely skirting one revenant's reaching arms while a second finished toppling the bookshelves. Books crashed resoundingly to the floor and Shadow could feel the table lifting beneath her. She jumped back to the floor with a sword-wielding revenant only a breath behind her.

There was nowhere left to run.

Shadow scrambled over fallen furniture, glancing around desperately. The revenant was closing on her fast. Donya was doing fine against the two she battled, but there was no hope she could help. Blade was fighting, hard-pressed, against two more, the short sword and Shadow's dagger in her hands.

Even as Shadow ducked recklessly around a table, only a moment ahead of her pursuer, movement caught the corner of her eye. Baloran had apparently abandoned the revenants in the yard for the present, for his attention was fully on them, and he held something in his hand, something long and glowing. He raised the wand, pointing the rod at Blade, and opened his mouth.

Without thought, Shadow's hand grasped a dagger at her

belt and released it. Slowly, endlessly it spun, end over end, a glistening black blade drinking the magelight flickering through the room.

The dagger buried itself almost hilt-deep in Baloran's chest just as white heat seared through Shadow's back. Baloran looked down with amazement at the jet-black hilt protruding from his body as Shadow looked numbly down to see the end of the revenant's sword emerge red-stained from her belly, sliding outward with a hideous grating sound. Then it stopped where it was and she heard the revenant collapse behind her.

As she fell, interminably, she could hear Baloran's screams.

They echoed for a long, long time.

Flutter of movement. Donya, seeking frantically through the vials and potions scattered over the floor.

"Help me, damn you!" she screamed at Blade. "There may be a healing potion here!"

Shadow tried to chuckle. She doubted it. Healing potions weren't Baloran's style.

Blade looked unhurriedly at Donya. She pulled the black dagger from Baloran's chest—his eyes were still open, wide with horror, his mouth gaping in a soundless scream—and flipped it into the air. She caught it.

"No," she said. "There is none."

She knelt beside Shadow. "I should let Blackfell drink your soul," she said coldly. "Baloran was mine."

"Sorry," Shadow croaked. "I thought better him than you. Foolish of me, wasn't it?"

"Very." Blade glanced up as Donya knelt beside Shadow. "Turn her over and hold her."

"She'll start bleeding heavily as soon as you pull that out," Donya protested even as she obeyed, wincing at Shadow's grimace of pain as she was moved. "Maybe there's time—the elves aren't too far away—"

Mercifully Shadow blacked out after the first raw agony

as Blade pulled, but only briefly. Donya's face wavered back in, wet with unheeding tears as she cradled Shadow to her. Blade was ripping Donya's shirt away from the wound. The demon squatted impassively beside her, and Shadow wondered briefly if Blade had decided to give her to it after all.

"How about some wine?" Shadow gasped to Donya.

"I don't think you should try—"

"Can't hurt," Shadow grinned feebly.

"You'll be all right," Donya said hurriedly. "If we bandage you tightly, make a litter—"

"Come on, Doe," Shadow croaked. "You're a lousy liar. Wine."

Donya bit her lip but held the wineskin to Shadow's mouth. Shadow choked down one mouthful and coughed out the rest; Donya took the skin away.

"Shadow—" Donya began, ruthlessly knuckling away tears. Her hand smeared blood over her face.

"Oh, be silent, both of you," Blade snapped. "You make me ill."

"You!" Donya's face contorted with fury. "This is your fault—"

"Get her out of my way," Blade said coldly to the demon.

Blackfell did not move, but Donya abruptly vanished. Shadow heard a crash from the other end of the room, and Donya's frantic cursing. She might have laughed if the sudden drop to the floor had not sent a new spear of agony through her. The world wavered briefly.

"Good enough," Blade said impassively. "Prop her up from that side."

Shadow groaned as they forced her upright. The feeling of liquid warmth flowing down her belly and the smell of blood made her suddenly nauseous.

"Vomit on me," Blade warned, "and you will be in more pain than you are now."

She laid one hand flat over Shadow's heart, the other over

the wound in her belly. Shadow felt Blackfell's cold hands press against the entry wound at the back.

"Now," Blade said.

Shadow screamed as cold fire seared through her back to front, more painful than the sword thrust and infinitely longer. The moment seemed to stretch out in time until Shadow thought she would die of the pain alone.

Abruptly it ceased.

Blade and Blackfell removed their hands at the same time, letting Shadow collapse where she was. She lay on her face on the stone, gasping for breath, her body tingling furiously, wondering what further tortures she might expect to endure before she could finally die in peace.

More furniture crashing, then Donya's gentle hands turned her over. Shadow heard her friend's gasp, then a wondering touch on her belly. She forced herself to look.

Blood was all over her, dried, drying, and still sticky wet, but none was new. On her belly was a thin red scar, fading to pink at the edges.

Despite Donya's restraining hands, Shadow pushed herself upright to grope at her back. The scar there was tender, and there was a fierce ache when she moved, but the wound was firmly closed.

Shadow groped for the wineskin Donya had put down earlier and swallowed wine and wine and wine, letting it spill down her chin. Her clothes could hardly suffer more.

Blade was getting up, but she froze when Donya laid a strong, callused hand on her arm. Blade's eyes narrowed dangerously and Shadow swallowed hard, glancing at the demon.

"Thank you," Donya said quietly. "Whatever magic you did, thank you."

"It is nothing to do with you, High Lord's daughter," Blade said impassively. She pulled her arm free of Donya's grasp and moved to retrieve her knives. The black dagger was back in her belt. After a moment she walked to stand silent over Baloran's body.

Donya frowned, and Shadow spoke quickly to distract her.

"I'm not sure I'm going to be good for any riding," she said humbly. "Undignified as it may be, think you can find something to make a litter?"

Carefully, Donya hugged her.

"Bet on it," she laughed through her tears. "Stay still here while I look. If necessary, the guards and I will break up the furniture. I'm sure the men will be more than delighted to wreck the place."

Shadow ignored the order and as soon as Donya was gone, she used a table to pull herself painfully to her feet. She limped over to stand beside Blade.

"No healer, huh?" she said.

Blade shrugged. "You healed yourself. I but gave you the life energy to do it. It took most of what you had paid me," she added sourly. "Stupid of me, I suppose."

"Very," Shadow grinned.

"Life for life," Blade shrugged. "At least we are even on that score." Her lips tightened as she gazed at Baloran. "But this . . ."

"Life's better than revenge," Shadow suggested.

"Is it?"

Something in Blade's tone made Shadow looked sidewise at her, and she felt a pang of something like pity. The assassin's face was as impassive as ever, but her eyes were empty: too empty.

"Maybe his books—" Shadow mused.

Blade glanced at her. "What are you babbling about?"

"Well, all those books," Shadow said. "I mean, he learned the magic to make the dagger from them, didn't he? Maybe a powerful enough mage could find a way to break it. He said there might be other mages more skilled at bindings than he. I don't know. You can buy almost anything with enough coin, and Fortune knows there's enough here to sell."

Blade glanced back toward the library.

"It would take months to puzzle them through," she said.

"You could take them with you," Shadow suggested. "Hire a mage. I could recommend one to you. Discreet if not cheap."

"You are the greedy one who brought the extra horse," Blade said coldly. "Not I."

"Yes, I brought the extra one," Shadow agreed. "I won't be riding either of them, it seems."

Blade let out a bark of contemptuous laughter.

"You could carry little treasure back if you burdened your beasts with those books," she sneered.

"Got any Dragon's Blood left?" Shadow asked casually. "I could use a taste."

Blade mutely held out Shadow's crystal flask. A little blood stained one side. Blade uncorked it and handed it to Shadow.

Shadow sipped, coughed, and handed it back. She glanced around the room at the arcane treasures there and sighed.

"Ah, who needs treasure?" she shrugged.

NINE

"Are you all right?" Donya asked worriedly, checking the travois for the fifth time. "Did I get the straps too tight?"

"No, I'm fine," Shadow said cheerfully. She patted the two wineskins Donya had tied in behind her. "Just fine."

Donya had to laugh back. "Easy stages," she said firmly. "A nice slow march along the Sun Road and then we'll let the guard go their own way while the elves take you in style and comfort through the Heartwood. There'll be healers there, and by the time we get back to Allanmere the messengers will have reached Auderic, and you can recover at the palace. And by *that* time I'll have sat with the Council of Churches under truthspell and gotten them settled down again."

"Fortune favor me, Doe, you're being ridiculous," Shadow said comfortably. "I could almost ride back now, and there's no need to take weeks about it, you know. The Guild's waiting for me. Aubry's come to some grief by now, bet on it, or he'll have stolen the entire Guild treasury and run off with it."

"It doesn't matter," Donya grinned. "You're alive, you'll steal another treasury's worth. Just as long as it's not the *palace* treasury. I think I'll have Auderic potion you again, just to be sure."

"What, rob you?" Shadow said innocently. "Poor, feeble me?"

Blade snorted.

"Chain down the foundations, then," she said contemptuously. She was fastening the last of the books to Shadow's unhappy roan and the placid bay.

"Take good care of them," Shadow grinned. "They're not as sturdy as yours. And please, please don't eat them."

Blade raised one eyebrow, and for a moment Shadow thought she saw a corner of Blade's mouth twitch, just a little.

Donya tied the last knot on the harness, glanced at Blade, and hesitated. She gave the horse an absentminded pat, cleared her throat awkwardly, and stepped forward.

Blade's eyes narrowed warily.

"I—" Donya glanced at Shadow, then said stiffly, "I never saw you. I don't know who you are."

Blade chuckled a little. "Fair enough, High Lord's daughter. And in return, know that it will delight me as much as you if we never meet again."

Donya grinned weakly. "I'll agree to that."

Blade stepped to the side of the travois and gazed dispassionately down at Shadow.

"Doe, why don't you go talk to the guard and make sure they're ready," Shadow suggested. "I want to talk to Blade alone for a bit."

Donya frowned slightly, but nodded.

"All right," she said. "But not too long. We need to start back." She moved away to join the men.

"So you are to come away with nothing for all your trouble?" Blade asked.

"Oh, I wouldn't say *nothing*," Shadow sighed. "I've got that jar of stuff you gave me in the laboratory, and Donya packed away a few of the wands and such that she thought might be worth something to some mages back in town. The guards are taking some back for us, too, those of them who still have horses. Doesn't amount to much."

"That," Blade said acidly, "is what comes of foolishly giving your horses to another. But I will at least go so far as to pay you for them and avoid any further indebtedness to you. Debts owed to you, I have found, will cost me dear."

She tucked a pouch into Shadow's pack.

"I also visited Baloran's treasure," she said, her expression softening slightly. "It is fitting that he pay for your horses."

"True enough," Shadow chuckled. "But I wish you'd come back to Allanmere with us, or at least take the Sun Road around the forest with—"

"With the guard?" Blade chuckled mirthlessly. "I think not. I will not strain your noble friend's generous ignorance to the breaking. No, I will return as I came, through the swamp."

"All alone?" Shadow asked worriedly.

"Not precisely." Blade patted the ebony horse at her side.

"Hmm. I'm wasting my time worrying about you," Shadow grinned. "And I'm not Donya, anyway, to play big sister."

She was silent for a moment. "Blade," she said at last, "are you *ever* going to tell me where you came from? And where you got those scars?"

Blade scowled. "And if I choose not to," she growled, "I suppose you will simply pry about until you have dug up my every secret to satisfy your insatiable curiosity."

"Exactly," Shadow grinned.

Blade was silent for a long time, so long that Shadow was sure Blade would tell her nothing, but at last she nodded.

"I do not know whether my folk came to Allanmere's swamps before the elves took the forest, or after," she said. "It mattered not, for they avoided the swamp and we avoided the woods with equal fervor. We were a solitary people, not much inclined even to the company of each other. When elves or, later, humans entered our lands, we killed them if the swamp or its other denizens did not do it for us. We spied on the elves a bit, such as we could from the edge of the swamp. My people had no name for ourselves—we were kin, and the others were strangers. That was enough.

"When the barbarians poured down from the north we did not know it," Blade said, "nor would we have cared. We did not care how strangers killed each other, and no one would have wanted our lands. But a few of the invaders came to the swamps, hoping to forge a road through to Allanmere upon which they would not encounter the elvan patrols and could bypass Allanmere's defenses. Some of them stumbled upon us in the homes we had taken, the homes built so long ago by those mysterious folk who had come before.

"The invaders thought us allied with the humans and elves," Blade continued. "Many of us they killed. Some they took for questioning and . . . amusement. I was one such. I was fortunate, perhaps, for the barbarians found me not too ugly for their enjoyment, so I was able to escape scarred, but alive. What remained of my people had, in the meantime, fled before the barbarians to Allanmere, to plead for sanctuary. The humans saw their strange forms and thought them part of the invading force. They slaughtered what remained of my folk, shooting them with arrows from the wall or pouring burning oil down upon them. Even Allanmere's mages brought their magic down upon my hapless folk. It was ironic because it was the presence of my folk, whom the barbarians refused to believe were not allied with the humans, which in the end convinced the invaders not to attempt an approach through the swamp.

"I had survived, but I was alone," Blade said at last. "I could not remain in the swamp with the rotting corpses of my kin for company, and there was nowhere for me to go. I had picked up some Old Olvenic and what little my folk knew of the elves, and I fled to the forest, but the elves drove me forth. So I went as close to the city as I could without being seen. I took my knife to my own flesh,

carving away that which would betray me to the humans.
Clothing and bandages disguised what the knife could not
remove.

"For a few years I lived in Allanmere, living on the
fringes and in the dark places," Blade continued. "I found
it easy to kill for pay. What cared I for the lives of non-kin?
And I took pleasure in killing those who had taken part in
slaughtering my folk. I felt a responsibility to live on. I was,
after all, the last. One day I heard a rumor of Baloran's
dagger, the dagger which would grant longevity to its
possessor. I thought it a fine revenge to steal his immortality.
The rest you have guessed yourself. Now my body is no
longer my own, no more my soul."

Shadow was silent. She did not know what to say.

"Oh, do not look at me so," Blade snapped. "I have no
use for your pity, no more than your friendship. Let it be
enough that we have used each other to some profit and we
part without enmity."

Shadow grinned as she saw Donya returning. "If that's
enough for you, that's enough for me," she chuckled. "But
I'll remember your dancing kindly, and your liquor, whatever you think of me. And so I'll just say good-bye, have a
good time, and I'll see you in Allanmere soon."

"Not if I see you first," Blade grumbled.

"Why, Blade!" Shadow laughed. "From you, a jest!
Why, next you'll be drumming at a tavern while I sing and
dance and—"

She caught the pained expressions on both Blade's and
Donya's faces and chuckled.

"Well, maybe I'll let someone else sing," she conceded.

"And your dancing days are through for a time," Donya
said firmly. "And that time grows longer with every
moment we delay."

"All right, all right," Shadow sighed. She checked the
wineskins again. "Wretched coming here, sore going home,
but at least this time I can keep my feet dry."

She reached out her hand to Blade.

"Fair journey," she said. "And I *will* see you again. I still owe you a bow, after all."

Blade looked at the hand, half smiled contemptuously, and turned away. Silently she mounted her black steed, grasped the leads of the heavily laden roan and bay, and rode south without glancing back.

"I cannot imagine," Donya said exasperatedly, "what kind of a traveling companion she'd make."

Shadow laughed. "Quiet, Doe, and altogether too somber, but never boring; I can't deny her that. But just think! Even if it's just for a little while through the Heartwood, it'll be just you and me again!"

"Now, *that's* a happy prospect," Donya agreed. "And thanks be to the gods, you're not going to be able to wait on me."

"Oh?" Shadow asked curiously.

"Never mind," Donya said grimly. "You'll understand by the time we get to the forest."

She glanced at what remained of the guard, waiting a respectful distance away.

"Well, Captain Oram?" she called. "Shall we find our way home?"

"Aye, my lady," he called back. "With a good will indeed!"

The guard fell in behind the horse. Shadow hoped that the road would be smoother than the overland track they were following; she could already tell that every bump would be making itself felt. To distract herself, she took a few hearty swigs of wine.

As she tucked the wineskin back into the straps, she noticed the pouch that Blade had tucked into her pack. Curious, she pulled it out and opened it.

Inside the pouch was the largest diamond Shadow had ever seen—a little larger than the last joint of her thumb, with the faintest straw-gold tint.

"Well, Fortune favor me," Shadow murmured with

astonishment. The thing was probably worth the total of the Guild treasury, if not more.

"What's that?" Donya asked, falling back as Captain Oram moved forward to take the reins from her.

Shadow folded her hand over the stone, grinning.

"Just a souvenir," she said. "From a friend."

363